BEST CANADIAN STORIES
2021

BEST
CANADIAN
STORIES

EDITED BY
DIANE SCHOEMPERLEN

2021

BIBLIOASIS
WINDSOR, ONTARIO

FIRST EDITION
ISBN 978-1-77196-435-7 (Trade Paper)
ISBN 978-1-77196-436-4 (eBook)

Edited by Diane Schoemperlen
Copyedited by Allana Amlin
Cover and text designed by Gordon Robertson

 Canada Council   Conseil des Arts    ONTARIO | ONTARIO
for the Arts   du Canada   CREATES | CRÉATIF

 Canada   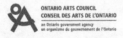 ONTARIO ARTS COUNCIL
CONSEIL DES ARTS DE L'ONTARIO
an Ontario government agency
un organisme du gouvernement de l'Ontario

Published with the generous assistance of the Canada Council for the Arts,
which last year invested $153 million to bring the arts to Canadians throughout
the country, and the financial support of the Government of Canada. Biblioasis
also acknowledges the support of the Ontario Arts Council (OAC), an agency
of the Government of Ontario, which last year funded 1,709 individual artists
and 1,078 organizations in 204 communities across Ontario, for a total of
$52.1 million, and the contribution of the Government of Ontario through
the Ontario Book Publishing Tax Credit and Ontario Creates.

PRINTED AND BOUND IN CANADA

CONTENTS

INTRODUCTION
Diane Schoemperlen

> The short story still has the flavour of a report from the
> front lines of history and existence.
>   — Aleksandar Hemon,
>   *Best European Fiction 2010*

> Who were we, and why did we live? What is a story and
> how might it be reimagined, opened up, transformed to
> accommodate all we've seen, all we've been hurt by, all
> that's been given, and all that's been taken away?
>   — Carole Maso,
>   *Break Every Rule: Essays on Language, Longing, and
>   Moments of Desire*

When the first edition of this series of annual anthologies
came out in 1971, I was still in high school and just beginning
to discover the wonders and the power of the short story. By
the time I was in university I was hooked, thoroughly smitten
by the early story collections of Alice Munro—*Dance of the
Happy Shades; Lives of Girls and Women; Something I've Been
Meaning to Tell You;* and *Who Do You Think You Are?*—and

1

Joyce Carol Oates—*By the North Gate; Upon the Sweeping Flood; The Wheel of Love;* and *Where Are You Going, Where Have You Been?* I have been reading, writing, and loving short stories ever since. I've also had a long relationship with this series, proud to have my own stories appearing in the 1987, 1990, and 2008 editions. And now I am honoured to be the guest editor for this, the fiftieth edition of *Best Canadian Stories.*

I suspected this would be a challenging task when I took it on and I was not wrong.

My job was to choose what I considered to be the fifteen best stories (plus another fifteen notable stories) written and/ or published by Canadians in print and online journals in the year 2020. My definition of the word "Canadian" was broad: born in Canada and still lives here; born in Canada and now lives elsewhere; born elsewhere and now lives in Canada; born elsewhere and still lives elsewhere but spent some significant part of their lives in Canada. Due to my own regrettable limitations as a unilingual person, I was only able to read stories available in English. Between the end of July 2020 and the end of May 2021, I looked at close to a thousand stories that appeared in twenty-four print journals and twenty-four online journals, plus another twenty stories that were submitted directly to me. In those ten months I was as thorough as I could possibly be in my reading but even with all of that, I know there were probably other stories that I didn't discover and would have loved if I had.

When I began reading for this anthology at the end of July 2020, here in Canada we were about five months into the COVID-19 pandemic. All of our lives had been upended— in relatively minor and manageable ways for some, but in irreparable and catastrophic ways for so many others. At home alone with my three cats, I was perpetually anxious and exhausted, grieving for the entire world. Time had gone all stretchy and weird. I often didn't know what month it was, never mind which day of the week. I was an early adopter of the now ubiquitous mask and at the beginning of April, long before it became mandatory, I started wearing one every time I left the house, even just to put out the garbage. In those early COVID days, I was not accomplishing much of anything and not even feeling guilty about it: taking reasonably good care of myself and the cats and the house seemed like accomplishment enough on any given day. I did not take up yoga, meditation, or running. I did not bake a single loaf of bread.

When I wasn't posting cat pictures on Facebook, texting with my son, doomscrolling, or playing silly games on my phone, I was watching *90 Day Fiancé* and *The Bachelor*, these and other reality TV shows having absolutely nothing to do with reality and thus somehow mitigating the overwhelming *unreality* of our actual reality—if you know what I mean. I was also obsessively tracking the numbers locally, provincially, nationally, and internationally. With my need to know what was happening slugging it out daily with my need to protect my mental health, I was unable to look away from the news even though I knew I should. And it wasn't just the increasingly alarming COVID news—it was one tragic and terrifying thing after another. To name just a few: there was the devastating evidence of climate change causing more and more extreme weather events all over the world; there was Canada's worst mass shooting in Portapique, Nova Scotia, in April, and then the murder of George Floyd by police in Minneapolis, Minnesota, in May and all that came after. The whole world as we knew it was in upheaval. It was impossible not to wonder if these were the end times. Was this the apocalypse now?

My favourite Facebook meme of that time was a picture of the red Breaking News banner with the words "Good lord what the fuck now" across the bottom. At least there was one thing to be thankful for: the murder hornets never came.

Unlike many of my literary friends, I found myself unable to write. In the face of their exuberant productivity, this felt like a shameful moral failure on my part and did indeed generate rather large doses of guilt and frequent full-blown bouts of despair. I turned instead to my other creative work and made collages about the pandemic and shared them on Facebook where they were purchased as quickly as I could produce them. This process of creating and sharing brought me a great measure of relief from the misery.

Although my love of reading had helped me through many crises in my life, now I found that it too had mostly deserted me. I was lost and unmoored without it. This sudden lethargy and lack of interest regarding all things literary was disturbing to say the least. My concentration and attention span had dwindled to the point where I no longer had the bandwidth to read more than ten or twenty pages at a stretch. As a person who has read two or three books a week for the last forty years, now it took me two or three weeks to read *one* book, and then often not all the way to the end.

My brain was so foggy that it wasn't until that first box of literary journals arrived in July 2020 that I finally realized short stories could be the perfect antidote to this problem. I dipped in eagerly and my literary lethargy began to lift. More boxes of print journals continued to arrive in the coming months, as well as many files in digital form. Me being me, I found great satisfaction in setting up a system of multiple lists, charts, and spreadsheets in an attempt to keep all this reading organized and to give myself the illusion of having everything under control.

I read through the summer. The pandemic continued: lockdown, reopening, lockdown, reopening, repeat. Sometimes things got better but it was never long before they got worse again. I lost track of which wave we were in. I grew increasingly furious at those who would not follow the safety protocols. Disturbing news on other fronts also continued apace.

The few things that remained constant and predictable from one day to the next were uncertainty, loneliness, frustration, exhaustion, and the unnerving sense of living in a very long sci-fi horror movie.

In September my work as an online mentor for the Humber School for Writers resumed. I continued to read for the anthology through the fall and early winter, squeezing it in now around everything else that needed to be done. I was beginning to feel overwhelmed, not only by the amount of reading required, but increasingly and more importantly, by the necessity of having to *judge* each story, to pick and choose from so many good ones when there were so few that could actually be included in the book. I read through the Christmas holidays. Thanks to COVID, this would be the first Christmas I had ever spent entirely alone. Having never been a big fan of Christmas, I convinced myself that this might actually be a pleasant change. It was not.

In January 2021, I bought myself a belated Christmas present: George Saunders' brilliant new book, *A Swim in a Pond in the Rain: In Which Four Russians Give A Master Class on Writing, Reading, and Life*—the four Russians here being Tolstoy, Turgenev, Gogol, and Chekhov. This led me to begin reading the 13-volume set of Chekhov stories I had bought myself as a somewhat extravagant and ambitious Christmas present a decade earlier. I had dipped into this beautiful boxed set several times over the intervening years, but now I was determined to read the entire set. And I did.

As I write this introduction, I realize I have spent the last six months in an intense state of short story immersion, reading Chekhov every morning and stories for the anthology every afternoon, sometimes in the evening too. Still the pandemic and the surreal were never far from hand. On many April mornings, with the familiar and reassuring signs of spring outside and me happily settled in my reading chair with Chekhov, a cup of coffee, and a cat or two, there would come the sound of a helicopter flying low over my house, bringing COVID patients to the Kingston hospital from cities whose own hospitals were filled beyond capacity.

Reading Chekhov's stories written more than a century ago and all those brand-new "hot off the press" stories in tandem helped clarify what was I looking for in this anthology.

I wanted stories to which I felt an immediate connection in the first few sentences. In a short story there is no room for warming up the way there can be in a novel. In a short story, as in poetry, every word matters. This kind of immediate connection is akin to what people often say about love: when you find "the one," you will just *know*. Based on my own rather extensive experience with both love and stories, this advice is much more reliable when applied to stories.

I wanted stories that took risks—in voice, language, time, character, subject matter, point of view, form and structure, plot or the lack thereof. My own work has been described as "challenging the short story form." Over the years I have found that the short story is always up to that challenge and can be the perfect vehicle for taking chances. It is malleable, expansive, generous, flexible, and, as I have found, always amenable to innovation, evolution, and revolution. I wanted stories that would wreak havoc with conventions and expectations.

I wanted stories that, to paraphrase Raymond Carver in his fine essay "On Writing," carried news from the writer's world to mine and I wanted stories in which there was some feeling of mystery or menace, a sense of tension and things being set in relentless motion. I wanted stories that were more than one thing—stories that were both simple and complex, gorgeous and gruesome, sparse and loaded, humorous and heartbreaking.

I wanted stories that lingered in my mind long after they were read.

I have found all of this and more in the fifteen stories included here. Rather than attempt to "curate" my selections in some way, arranging them by theme or subject or style, I have chosen simply to put them in alphabetical order by author's last name. I've done this partly because I love the alphabet—after all, where would we writers be without it?—but mostly because I think this more impartial system of ordering will better replicate the sheer thrill of discovery that I felt as I read each one of them for the first time.

Whenever I read a book that excites me, I immediately want to spread the word and press it into the hands of everyone I know, saying, "You've got to read this so we can talk about it!" That's exactly how I feel about this book now that it's done.

Clearly, the short story is alive and thriving in the hands of Canadian writers. The best short stories are disruptive in all the best ways, diverse in all senses of the word, always looking back and leading us forward at the same time. As I write this introduction at the end of June 2021, I recognize and understand more deeply that the best short stories cannot be written in a vacuum. They must be written in the world, in the midst of a pandemic, in the midst of more horrifying news every day of the bodies of Indigenous children being found in unmarked graves at former residential school sites across Canada. They must be written in the midst of trauma and despair and anger and shame, as well as in the midst of whatever fleeting moments of peace and hope any of us can come by now.

The best short stories, like the fifteen featured here, will always bring us news of the world and the shape of things to come.

*

LET'S PLAY DEAD

Senaa Ahmad

There was a man, let's call him Henry VIII. There was his wife, let's call her Anne B. Let's give them a castle and make it nice. Let's give her many boy babies but make them dead. Let's give him a fussy way of being. Let's make her smart and sneaky, because it's such a mean thing to do.

Let's make it so she can't escape.

Let's seal the bottle, and shake it, and shake until our hands fall off.

*

It takes two swings to cut off her head. Everyone does their best to pretend that the first one didn't happen. In the awkward silence afterwards, the swordsman says something about mercy or justice, a strangely fervent soliloquy in French that might have made Anne herself emotional, but it's a touch long-winded, and no one's paying him any attention. And she's dead, so it's especially beside the point.

The ministers dither in the courtyard, chancing last looks, murmuring, *Exquisite mouth, just exquisite.* She is so beautiful, they agree, even beheaded.

Henry will return to the body later, when everyone's gone and what's left of her has been moved to the chapel. He will stand on the threshold, halfway between one momentous decision and the next. He will kneel on the dais beside her severed head and lay one ornately rubied hand along her frigid cheekbone. Maybe he will stay five minutes. Maybe he will stay thirty-five. Maybe he will cry softly, but it doesn't matter, because there isn't a nosy patron around to commission an oil painting for the textbooks, and it doesn't matter because she's dead, she's still very, very dead.

He will leave as furtively as he came, wiping his hand on his smock. Anne's headless body and bodiless head will be left to their own devices, her blood blackening, thickening on the ground, the gristle of her neck tougher with every minute. The clock ticks. Night falls.

It is her head that speaks first. It says, "Is he gone?"

Her body spasms, maybe a shrug, or maybe just a reflex.

Her head opens its eyes and looks this way, that way. It says, "It's over? It really worked?"

*

We don't need to stick around while her body crawls its way to her head and fits itself back together. Every excruciating inch of the stone floor is a personal coup, and every inch lasts the whole span of human history. It is slow. It is clumsy. The head falls off a couple of times. The body is floppy with atrophy. There is a lot of blood. She probably, definitely cries. It does not befit a queen.

*

He is reading the Saturday paper, still in his shirtsleeves, when she breezes in the next morning. The horizon of the paper lowers to the bridge of his nose. He is a man who wears his tension in the way of a beautifully tuned piano, and in this moment he vibrates at a bewildered middle octave.

"Anne," he says, at an absolute loss.

"Henry," she says, the picture of politeness.

She sits at the table. Not a hair out of place, not a leaky vein in sight. She butters her toast in four deft strokes. A servant steps out from the shadows to fill her teacup to the brim. It's all very serene, domestic. If it takes her a few tries to put her toast back on the plate, or if he dabs his napkin with a little extra violence, well, who can say. She slurps her tea, which they both know he hates. He hoists his newspaper back up. Like this, they go on.

*

Of course she knows what comes next. Let's not fib.

She is seized from her bed some weeks later, in a state of drowsy dishabille, the wardens bristling with royal braid. This night will have the consistency of a dream. The palace swims in sound and darkness. The youngest one, the boy or man who grips her arm with one rubbery fist and studiously avoids her gaze, reminds her of the sons she has lost in the womb. She wants to tell him, *Don't worry, the thing you're afraid of, the girl, the job, the rising cost of real estate in London, it will all work out someday—you'll see, it all comes to pass*, but he is leading her to her death, so it seems a bit impolite.

The cooks are baking down in the kitchen. The yeasty comfort of this aroma, which reminds her of the seam of volcanic heat that escapes when she cracks a fresh loaf, of a day opening beneath her, is too much. She shuts her nostrils. Her silk nightgown flaps at her ankles. When she can, she reaches out and touches the walls, the radiators, the edges of doorframes. Reminding herself that she is here, now, she is alive, that this dream is all too real. She can't falter yet. There's work to do.

A gibbet stands in the courtyard beneath a lonesome moon. They thread the noose around her neck with genteel care, snugly, even though the youngest one quakes every time his skin makes contact with hers. Up in the turret window, she sees Henry watching at a distance, as he does best. A coward in his big-boy breeches.

It is a quick death. The noose is tight. The drop is long. No one's trying to be cruel here. One person cries out but is quickly silenced. The wardens double-check, triple-check to make sure she's properly dead this time. From the courtyard to the turret, they flash a thumbs-up to Henry. He lets the curtain fall. This time, he does not visit her tenderly. It is done.

The wardens will return to their card games, all except the youngest one, who will mourn her without meaning to. He will simmer with sorrow for hours until, without warning to himself or others, he punches a wall so hard he fractures most of the knuckles in his right hand, leaving a fist-size whorl of buckled plaster as a signature.

And when she wakes up, hours later, on a slab of wintry marble in the royal morgue, it's with a broken neck and very little air in her lungs. She adjusts her neck the way she might correct a crooked hat—difficult without a proper mirror, but she manages. She tightens the belt on her flimsy nightgown and slips through the haunted halls, pausing only when she reaches the king's chambers. She doesn't knock. She doesn't crow or look for consolation, although the pang is there, and it feels unstoppable. Instead, with great effort, she continues on to her apartments, where she goes right back to bed. She is wiped, and the throb in her neck is telling her to conserve strength. But most of all, it is such a trivial insult to him, so small, so vicious, to fall asleep as soundly as she does this night.

*

For a time, it is quiet. Henry waits. He consults his advisers, who are just as baffled. He tries to get his head around the situation, but at least he has the good grace to do it far from her.

You will want to hear that Anne takes solace in these precarious days, so let's say that's true: she takes that trip she always meant to, an ethereal island resort where every day the indigo waters whisper *Get out, get out while you still can* and the jacarandas whistle a jaunty tune of existential dread. She cashes in her many retirement portfolios, she doesn't so much throw parties as fling them, handfuls of bacchanalia into those feverishly starlit nights.

Or: she digs her heels deep into the Turkish carpets of her palatial apartments and doesn't budge. In the bruised hours between dusk and midnight, she feels a joy so grandiose that it fills the empty canals and sidewalks within her. She takes to promenades around the gardens, drinking in the virtuous geraniums in their neat rows and the slightly ferocious hedge maze with its blooming thistles and uncertain corners. She grows sentimental about centipedes and spiders and wasps and belladonna and ragwort and nettles and every other hardscrabble weed, every pernicious pest. *I'm still here*, she says to the wasps, the centipedes, the belladonna, the ragwort. *I'm still here.*

The joy of the narrow escape is that it unfurls into hours, hidden doors that lead to secret passages of days, even if those days are numbered, even if she knows it. None of it is hers and it's all she's got. She loses herself, like a woman in a myth, unstuck in borrowed time, unravelling with possibility.

And yes, maybe she feels a few inches of gratitude for the armistice he has granted her. And yes, of course, the waiting days smother her, the twinned knowing and not-knowing what happens after, imagining Henry at every turn, cartoony with rage or puzzlement, but what is she to do?

*

After that, he drowns her himself. And who could blame him? If you want a job done right, you'd better know the end of this sentence. He comes upon her in the bath. He wraps his hands around her bare shoulders and thrusts her beneath the bathwater. Soap bubbles and air bubbles bloom in multitude. An artery in his skull skitters wildly. The water fights. The walls steam with tension.

She tries to thrash away from him, of course. She tries to defend herself, of course. But he's six foot two, built like a line-backer, and she is not. There is nothing more complicated here. He is not the first man to do this, or the wealthiest, or the angri-est. He certainly isn't the last. As they say, it's a tale as old as time.

Eventually the water stills. Her body floats. He sits on the brim of the tub, head bowed, the cuffs of his doublet dripping, his fingers pruning a gentle shade of violet. Up close, murder is a messy business, decidedly unroyal, too much flesh and screaming. He sits in wait—for how long, who knows. When the surface moves again and she sits up, feral-eyed and vomit-ing bathwater, he sighs.

"What do we do with you?" he says, not so much a ques-tion as a regret. And she has no answer, of course she has no answer.

*

It is he who helps her out of the tub, although she resists. He hands her the bathrobe, courteously studying the mosaic of the floor while she covers up. He helps her back to her rooms.

You will want her to scream at him, perhaps. To shove her house key through the soft wetness of his eye, to land a solid, bone-cracking punch to his solar plexus, or at the very least to kick him in his royalest of parts, but she has just survived death. She is alive. Today, that will have to be enough.

*

Anne's ladies never stray far. Where are they going to go? They hold their tongues. They massage their fists back into impas-sive hands. They, too, have intimate knowledge of the place between a rock and an even harder rock.

Sometimes they will perform small acts of metonymy. A pamphlet folded into a paper airplane is a clandestine invitation to the city. They will fetch her those darling meringue pastries if she is doleful, and so when they say, *We will bring you the French cookies,* it means *We are rooting for you to find a way.*

Or: an elegantly embroidered handkerchief means *I bayoneted this cloth nine thousand forty-two times and imagined it was the flesh of your enemies.* A pair of white gloves means *We will help you bury the bodies. We will not ask questions. We know you did what had to be done.*

If they tune up her automobile restlessly, it's to say, *Are you listening? We have a plan.*

A book of poems with no poems inside is this: *You are not defined by the tragedy of it. There is always one more page.*

They will nod with such enthusiasm that they black out, which means *Do you know how much we hate this?*

Sometimes they will weep in private, because there is too much to be said and nowhere to say it. Because they know that leaving is the most dangerous thing she can do. Because all they want is the impossible and is that really so much? Because this is one of the very few ways they can uncork their anger, and it is such a fine vintage, the very best. Because their fury is the scaffolding upon which their waiting lives are begotten, and it is so fathomless and pure, it clenches up their jaws and grinds their teeth into their gums. In this particular case, their tears mean *We will be your remembrance. We will salt the earth with the blood of our eyes so nothing can ever grow again.*

*

Henry is learning.

He gets crafty. He invents the portable long-barrelled firearm. Then he invents the firing squad. Then he invents acute ballistic trauma. Then he sends his wardens to find her.

But while he's busy doing all that, she's been busy, too, inventing: cardiopulmonary resuscitation. The telephone. The 911 call. First-response teams. Modern-day surgery. Organ transplants. Crash carts. Gurneys. Subsidized medicine. She improvises like it's the only thing she knows how to do.

It is ugly, obviously. There is quite a lot of blood and gore and spattered internal organs. But she lives. Still, she lives.

*

Lest you think it's all maudlin garden strolls and gallows touched by moonlight, let's admit that Anne and Henry still have their moments. Like the time a scullery maid starts a stovetop fire and trips the palace-wide alarm. All around the castle, the sprinkler systems kick in, first in the kitchens, then in the great hall, and then everywhere, misting porous manuscripts, Brylcreemed foreign dignitaries, the throne room, everyone on their toilets, Henry's collection of vintage cameras, and Anne in her finest silk pajamas, snoring over her watercolours. Still very much not dead.

She escapes to the nearest balcony. And as she wrings her ruined shirt and her hair in futility, a window creaks open and who should climb through but Henry, his arms filled with soaking scrolls almost as tall as himself. He sees her sodden in her nightclothes and begins to guffaw.

She says, "That's not very kingly," feeling hurt, and more vulnerable than she wants to be, and probably a little foolish.

He says, "Well, you don't look especially queenly," and drops the scrolls in a heap. She despairs at her reflection in the window.

"The gossip magazines are going to love this look," she says.

"Easy fix," he says. "Here." He sweeps up to the balcony's edge, blotting her from view of the courtyard. So close that she's immediately on high alert. She steps back. Every muscle clamped.

"You need more width," she says, with all the calm she can summon.

He begins to windmill his arms like a complete fool. He doesn't say a word, just churns his arms up and down with intense concentration. And to her own surprise, she starts to laugh. She can't help it. He does his best deadpan, smile uncracked, but it's there in the twitch of his eyebrows, the twinkle in his eye.

"What's your plan here?" she says.

"Trickery," he says, not missing a step. "Misdirection. Excellent upper-arm strength."

You may be thinking that this would be an opportune time to push him off the balcony, make it look like an accident, and maybe you wouldn't be wrong. But he's still the size of a world-class heavyweight boxer, and she is still most decidedly not. And yes, she's eager to please, and yes, even now, he can find ways to disarm her utterly. And yes, this moment, precious as it is, has a kind of power on its own, a force, and the ache of laughter in her abdomen will sustain her a few days longer. Do you really want to take that away from her?

*

It's easy to say that it becomes a game for him, and a game for her. In Anne's case, if it's a game, the game is Monopoly, her game piece is a pewter chicken with its head *décapité*, the banker is a scoundrel and a cheat, the properties disintegrate every time she lands on them, and the dice are made of fire. What game is this to him? If he's winning, does it even matter?

But for her, how's this for an alternative: on a spectral day in autumn, a cockroach tumbles across Anne's writing desk like a very squirmy, very small shooting star. It is swift, intrepid. In its wayward progress, it hemorrhages anxiety.

Its clumsy, heroic journey plucks the tenderest meat inside her. Is it any surprise that she sees something in the cockroach that hums on the same frequency as she does? She builds tranquil highways with her hands, one at a time, and is rewarded when the roach travels safely through. Her triumph is no small thing.

She hopes it is a girl cockroach, that the baseboards and the cracks in the wall are seething with her unhatched eggs, that beneath the floors the concrete is bulging with her magnificent cockroach babies. She hopes they are abundant and hungry. That every day, each year, the cockroaches and their cockroach babies encroach in an ever-expanding circle from their nest. That when civilization crumbles into the ground, and textbooks get chucked en masse into the sea, and all of this is done and gone—and it will be done, it will be gone, she's got to believe that the universe has a long memory and a short temper and that this, this is nothing—they will still be here, in the walls, under the floors, teeming, multiplying, ravenous, devouring, surviving.

*

He has his body servant stuff handkerchiefs down her throat. What you might call a reverse magic trick. Silk handkerchiefs, floral handkerchiefs, designer ones, handkerchiefs dipped in eau de cologne, ones that carry the perfume of another woman, while Henry lurks in the doorway, exultant.

It is such an absurd way to die that she begins to laugh, and once she starts laughing, it's too late, she can't stop. She even helps the servant stuff them down her throat. It is not pleasurable, by any means, but it bewilders him and leaves Henry stunned.

"Um, should I keep going?" the body servant is asking Henry, the last thing she remembers before she dies.

*

Sometimes he is fuzzy on the details. Sometimes he will forget and call her by the names of his other wives and she will have to correct him. He might leave her alone if she were some-body else, it's true. But she is unwilling to be forgotten.

"I'm Anne," she says impatiently. "*Anne*. Remember? Not Jane or Other Anne or Catherine. You haven't killed those ones yet."

*

He lines up everyone she has known, her mother and father, her dead brothers, her childhood friends, her nursemaid, her tutors, her grandmother, her priests, the snooty cousin she almost married, all the kids in high school who made fun of her. One by one, they tell her every mean thing they have ever thought about her.

"You're such a needy person," her grandmother says. "I often dread the sound of your approach."

"You're much less attractive than you think," says her snooty cousin.

"We always thought your jokes were kind of repetitive," her dead brothers confess.

"You probably shouldn't have started the English Refor-mation," one of the priests says.

"I didn't want another daughter," her mother admits.

"You *still* smell like farts," says one of the kids from school.

"I always thought you had so much potential," says a child-hood friend. "I wish I could take more pride in having known you."

It goes on like this for hours. In the centre, Anne, lovely Anne, poor Anne, with her hands over her face, bawling, full-on ugly-crying. Shoulders shuddering, snot-nosed, basically a mess. At some point, probably during her father's seven-min-ute monologue about everything they could've spent their fortune on if she hadn't been born, she will faint with grief and maybe dehydration, and the court physicians will not be able to revive her. Everyone goes home: her mother, father, dead brothers, and so on. She passes later in the evening, with little fanfare, most likely of a broken heart.

*

There is a version of her story where she doesn't die again and again and again.

There is a version of her story where she shivs him in his sleep.

There is a version where she is born in the future, and when she meets Henry at one of those rickety self-serious parties at Oxford, his discount-aristocracy vibes, prickly disposition, and fixation with his own poetry are clanging alarm bells. She walks away and never looks back.

There is a version where she gives birth to a daughter. In this version of the story, Anne still dies in the most ignoble and depressing of fashions: a sword, a Frenchman, a chopping block, gawking ministers, a wordless husband. It is her daughter who will avenge her mother—with the throne she takes by force, the wars she wages, the playwrights she patronizes, the papacies she outwits, the rebellions she crushes, the cults she accidentally spawns, the people she forgives, through all the many men she meets and never marries.

*

She wakes up one morning and the whole castle is closed for renovations. The imperial estates are empty and eerie. Set painters are giving the outer walls a fresh coat. A few crew members crawl on their hands and knees in the chapel, swabbing delicate graining details into the marble flagstones so they don't look like plastic. In the state room, a prop maker wheels away a vase, completely oblivious to her presence. He replaces it a few minutes later with an almost identical, slightly more era-appropriate vase.

When she passes Henry in the hallway, he's just as perplexed as she is.

But later that day, on instinct, he swipes a can of paint from the art department. He composes a sprawling landscape. A canyon, right in front of Anne's apartments. He's not the best artist, but what he lacks in talent, he makes up in cruelty. When she steps out of her room, she plunges right in, all the way to the bottom of the canyon, where she breaks her leg.

She tries to call for help. Of course she does. She yells until her voice is hoarse. Her leg is an unsteady line of fire beneath her. For days after, she can still hear the sound of the bone breaking.

And this time, yes, it's bad. She's hungry, thirsty, in tremendous pain. She is depleted from the ache of the last death, a grief she didn't know was still possible. She's worn down by his anger, his relentless need. There's a limit to what she can endure, maybe, and it doesn't seem so far away. She can't do this forever. Did you think she could do this forever?

Still, she looks for a way out. She tries to set the bone herself, with little success. She prays to her god for an answer. It would be better if she knew how to die, if she had the grace of a dead girl. But she is not a woman washed ashore at the start of a film, or arranged artfully in a back alley for the cameras to find. No, she's disorderly, desperate. There is skin beneath her fingernails, and throw-up on her T-shirt.

And do we want her to die? Do we want this to be the end? Isn't it better if she finds a miracle, a mystery machine swooping out of the sky to save her?

Think about it: Do you want her to be just another dead girl? Do you really, truly want her to die?

*

She does not die this time. One of the production assistants drops a permanent marker down the canyon by accident and Anne scrawls an amateurish ladder to freedom. Or, no, as everyone's packing up to leave, a decorator spies the velvet flag she's manufactured out of her French hood. He doesn't seem to understand who she is, but she bribes him to haul her out with two fat pearls.

Either way, it's definitely a miracle. Most unexpected. We'll leave it up to you.

*

On another day, she rolls over and looks at him.

"What?" he says.

"It doesn't have to be this hard, right?" she says. "We don't have to live like this."

He doesn't respond right away. He takes so long, she thinks he is considering the enormity of her question, that perhaps it has left him winded. She thinks maybe this is the moment he will realize how pointless it is, how hard she's trying, how much time he's wasted, how defeated they both are. Maybe he will say, *Huh, why didn't I ever think of that.*

But he doesn't answer, no surprise. He doesn't have anything to say. Maybe it's too obvious for words. Maybe he doesn't think she deserves a response. When he looks at her, she has the sense of a man who is making up his mind one way or another. A man who stares at a dead end and sees his opportunity.

*

Maybe you will want to look away for this part.

She will be taken to a laboratory, which, in the style of laboratories of the time and perhaps every laboratory in every time, feels a bit like the underbelly of a dungeon. Here she will be injected with a poison that liquefies her insides in a matter of hours. One of her captors will spill the poison on himself and this will derail the proceedings. They will perform an autopsy to confirm that she is dead. With a delicacy that is surgical, or at least very thorough, they will crack every bone in her body. They will take out her internal organs, still gooey and falling apart, and feed them to any nearby dogs, who may need a fair amount of persuading. She will wake several times, but never for long. There will be quite a lot of screaming, most likely, but you don't want to hear about that.

They will set her corpse on fire, and put the scorched bone fragments and teeth and shreds of flesh into a box. They will ship the box somewhere very far away, perhaps the remote island from earlier on. They will wrap the box in weights and cast it into the ocean. They will train a shark to develop a palate for mysterious boxes wrapped in weights so it can devour her remains. They will send a nuke from outer space to the precise coordinates of the shark. The bomb will vaporize the island, too, and everyone who lives there, a few thousand tidy deaths, but it's probably worth it.

*

They dispatch a courier to Henry immediately. The courier tells him, "She's dead," and Henry sags against the wall in relief. He spends the day in devout prayer. He waits a week or two for the obvious to happen. But no, she doesn't return.

He asks for extravagant bouquets to be delivered to her apartments, a mix tape of her favourites: English roses, bloody chrysanthemums, black tulips. He summons an architect to begin the blueprints for her memorial. He spends a whole day telephoning her parents and loved ones to break the news, with each call recalibrating his gravity, sorrow, and air of quiet suffering, depending on how much they care.

He will come to his bedroom later that night, a little weary, and there she will be, just like that. No explanation. She will be curled up in his favourite armchair like the slyest of cats, fast asleep, looking content. Fully intact, organs back in her body, insides unliquefied, most definitely *not* in a box, or a shark, or an ocean, or heaven, or hell.

*

Do you want to know how she did it?

Here's how she did it: her ancestors were microorganisms, and a few years later here she is. The secret is this: her great-grandparents were monkeys and now she can do long division. The only trick is to know better. Didn't anyone teach you to know better?

Here's how she did it: she was always rooting for the cockroach. No one mourns the cockroaches, the dust mites, the bacteria, the weeds, the worms. The chickens that endure their own beheadings. But she remembers. She remembers the things that survive and those that don't, and there are so many that don't, so very many.

Here's how she did it: she knows there's no difference between the entrance and the exit. It's not so difficult to turn around and walk right back in. Is it?

Here's how she did it: no one wants to see her die. Did you know it's that easy, to stay alive?

When you die, you should tell all the dead girls.

WHAT WOULD YOU DO?

Chris Bailey

When Clark moved the bed and Jane saw the rifle case there, she said, "I'm sorry about that."

Upstairs in a two-storey house in Hamilton, Ontario. A small room. Grey November light from a north-facing window. Vintage advertisements on the walls: Canada as *The Right Land for the Right Man*; one saying you should fly Northwest Orient Airlines. A framed print of three feathers etched so white lines show through blue and purple ink. Clark leaned the box spring against the wall.

He said, "I heard of a gun under the pillow. But under the bed."

If Jane were to turn around a dark line of sweat would be visible through her T-shirt.

Clark: "Guess you gotta keep it somewhere."

"Don't worry about it. Don't think about it. I didn't mean for you to see that." Jane put her hand to the mattress. "Let's get this in the other room."

She led the way into the hall, mattress sliding along a floor that went from the hardwood of the bedroom to short forest green carpet. Smiling faces in photographs helped paper the walls. Clark tried to not look at them.

"The freezer," Clark said.

"What?"

"Where I keep my gun. The freezer. Safe and sound right next to the heroin."

"I thought he took it," she said. "I could've sworn I saw him go with it to the truck when he left. It's deer season."

Clark had never hunted. He grew up in North Lake, PEI, and so he fished. That was how you made a living, put food on the table. All he saw it as. There were guys who enjoyed it. Hauling back nets and getting a ton of herring in a night, the saltwater air freezing in their nostrils when at the lobster come spring. In summer, people came from all over to fish bluefin tuna. Men felt like men standing next to a thousand-pound fish strung up from its tail, blood dripping out its mouth and pooling in the cracked and split cement at their feet. Men feeling like men by taking a life.

Jane knew all this. Knew about Clark Prosper's childhood. They'd been together a few years and were at the point where things they talked about rested in the past. Remember when such-and-such a thing happened, when so-and-so said this. Clark was unaccustomed to this familiarity but not against it. He had eased into an approximation of domesticity that surprised him. There was a time when what they talked about was happening or had yet to happen.

Her family has a hunting cabin. Sore spot for Jane: she was born during the season, and her dad and uncles missed her birthday every year to hunt in the coming cold. As a woman, she would never inherit any part of the cabin.

Jane and Clark didn't live together, but Clark liked helping out. Fix a faucet, change a bulb. Do some lifting. There was pleasure in this. As though him simply taking an end of a mattress was a profession of love. As though emptying the dishwasher or filling it, running a broom across the floor or taking the trash out held all he felt for Jane. Love letters written in things done.

When they got the mattress into the room, Clark went and pulled apart the old wooden bed frame. Pegs rotten, boards split. An IKEA job, he figured. He thought of moving the rifle case but decided not to touch it. That would be, he felt, an invasion of privacy. He used an Allen key and struck at the frame with the palm of his hand. A hammer would make a mess of things. He took two pieces at a time down the stairs and out the door and set them by the curb. Late afternoon, yet the windows in each house were dark. A nice neighbourhood not far from downtown, not far from the escarpment to the south. Busy, yet quiet road. What kind of place was this that no neighbours looked out to see what everyone was up to? He'd seen an old guy drink coffee and read a paper on sunny summer mornings, but that was it. The man was in his house that day or gone somewhere. They had never spoken. Clark had waved once and the man scratched at his belly.

A bus stopped nearby. No one got on, one person got off, walking in the same direction the bus travelled. One of those streets where, when the sun shined and the air was hot, homeowners paid other people to mow their grass, plant and tend their flowers. Clark had never spent time in such a place before Jane, it being reserved for movies and TV shows where everyone drinks their hard liquor neat or on the rocks, and there's always ice waiting to be used. His father paid him for chores when he was younger. Nothing much. A few dollars. Until he didn't.

Noah Prosper, in the past: "I shouldn't have to pay ya. You should be doing things out of the goodness of your heart, not with your hand out."

Clark found Jane sitting on the bed in the room they'd moved the mattress to. In the time it took him to take the frame apart and lug it out, she had rearranged the room and dressed the bed. There were teddy bears at its head, dolls on a nightstand nearby. Her daughter's room. Clark had met Jane's daughter and they got along well. She thought he was funny and Clark was surprised at how easily fond of her he was.

Clark: "You work fast."

"They'll be here in a few days," Jane said. "My mom, if things aren't just so."

"She'll be after you. I remember you saying."

He sat next to her. He wanted to say something. Wanted to tell her he loved her. Love was a grand thing. Something worth pursuing, worth professing. He believed he loved Jane. Not the first time he saw her, no. But the first time she smiled at him. Almost secretive. That smile was all it took, there being something in the look she gave him that Clark could never put his finger on. She called him a romantic, ragged on him, but it did not lessen the feeling.

Jane: "What do you think?"

"Looks nice."

"That doll, the Ringo Starr? I got that when I was her age. There are collectible colouring books I have I think I'll let her use."

What Clark thought: that's money down the drain. He thought this and immediately felt shitty about it and did his best to correct his way of thinking which he knew was really his father's way of thinking.

"It's a sweet thing," he said, "you sharing those with her."

"When she gets back with Mom, I think they'll both like doing it. Mom was always creative. You should see her with Cat."

The bedroom window faced south. Outside: a willow tree bent toward the house. Light trickled in, sun setting. He put an arm around her. She looked at him and said something and he said something, and then they were kissing. Making out like teenagers. This was what they would both remember, her kissing him on her daughter's bed and her saying, "I'm sorry. I can't. We can't," but not stopping, kissing him and between kisses he said, "I don't see why not," despite knowing why, both of them knowing and neither caring about whose face was smiling with her in photos on the walls, about the ring she wore that Clark did not put on her finger, and then their clothes were lost and they were moving together, with each other, against each other, her saying his name and him saying something like "Oh my god" and "I can't believe this." Months since they were together last.

Afterwards they stood in the kitchen. She poured him bourbon over ice. She had a half-glass of water on the go.

"I'm sorry," she said.

"You keep apologizing like you wronged me," he said. "You haven't."

"In my daughter's bed."

"Well, we know it'll hold her."

He sipped his drink. Him at the counter by the stove, her by the sink, arms folded over her chest. She looked small to him. She'd been saying for months how she needed to lose weight but she always looked small to Clark. He never told her for fear she'd think he was lying or attempting to placate her. His face not as honest as the rest of him.

"He got violent, you know. Not Michael, but my first husband," she said. "One of the last times I saw him was in the back window of a cab. He was chasing after it. I kept thinking, what if he catches up. What will he do?"

"I'm glad you're here. You're safe."

"What would you do?" she said. "If you found out your wife was going behind your back. Would you hit her with a shovel? Beat her? Shoot her?"

"I might have a word with the fella she was with. A real terse word."

"You can't know until it happens. Passion. They call that a crime of passion. Like an act of God channelled through a person. People get away with it."

Clark thought about the green of the rifle case. In his mind it was dark against the floorboards of the room upstairs.

Clark: "You don't have to worry about that anymore."

"Men want to hurt you," Jane said. "They want to kill you when they're jealous."

In the driveway, an engine rumbled. Clark set his drink on the counter. Stepped past Jane into the hall near the entry. Headlights through half-closed curtains.

Clark said, "You expecting someone?"

He watched the lights go out. Listened for the sound of a truck door closing.

FACSIMILE

Shashi Bhat

"I'm originally from Halifax," I type, and then delete. "Halifax, born and raised," I type, and then delete. "I used to be a high-school teacher," I type, and then delete. It's 3:30 p.m. at Uncommon Grounds, my favourite coffee shop in Halifax because of how big the scones are. My laptop is open in front of me—a Dell Inspiron I ordered on sale last month—and with one hand I'm crumbling my cheddar-chive scone, while with the other I work on my dating profile. I wipe crumbs on a napkin. I upload a photo of myself taken this summer. In it, I'm standing on the Halifax waterfront, smiling blandly. A tall ship casts a shadow over me, its spars decorated with festive, multicoloured pennant garlands. I delete the image, then open the file in Photoshop. I search online for a photo of a shark, extract it from its background, and paste it into my photo. I clone stamp and blur and filter until the shark looks like it's really there, eager-jawed in broad daylight, leaping over my head toward the ship. I save the file and upload it as my profile picture. I get up, put my empty plate in the bin for used dishes, and head to the bathroom. I pee, hold the flush down as instructed by a hand-scrawled sign above the toilet, and wash my hands. I walk back to my table. My laptop is gone.

As a Haligonian, I trust other Haligonians. Maybe not every Haligonian, but Haligonians as a group. Halifax is a city where everybody's on a first-name basis with Glen the busker who plays the accordion from his electric wheelchair on a corner of Spring Garden Road; where folks wave back at the Harbour Hopper (an amphibious tourist vehicle full of Americans on a cruise ship stop); where a city bus driver strums a ukulele to entertain passengers at long red lights; where Global News featured a story about masked men wandering the city performing random acts of kindness; where the youth-run social enterprise and community garden from an economically deprived area appears on *Dragons' Den*, wins an investment, and the whole city cheers and shows support by buying their fresh herb salad dressing at Atlantic Superstore. I always thought Haligonians were watching my stuff when I went to the bathroom.

There's a student sitting a couple tables down. I ask him whether he saw anybody take it. He pulls out one earbud and says, "Wha?" I repeat my question, but he says he didn't see anything. Odd that my handbag is still there. It's possible the thief didn't spot it hanging off the back of the chair, beneath my sweater. Perhaps they assumed from the quality of the bag itself that there was nothing in it worth taking. Perhaps they didn't have enough time.

I take the bus to my parents' house in the North End, and it stops by a high school. A big group of students get on. Summer school. It's been months since I've been in such proximity to so many teenagers. I feel acutely thirty-one years old. Everyone has a backpack on. In front of me are two girls in high-cut soccer shorts that expose their splotchy thighs. On my left stand a boy and girl mid-conversation. I can't see their faces because they're on my left and I don't want to turn and look, but the girl's backpack is in my periphery. It dangles a gaggle of anime charms—a squat pink bird with black pupils, a doll with an aggressive expression and blue painted-on hair. I wonder at what age she will decide to retire these to the back of a desk drawer.

"So what would you say are the flaws in my personality?" asks the girl.

"Flaws?"

"Yeah, I want to know what you think."

"You're not confident in yourself," the boy says. "And that makes you awkward around other people. It shows that you're not confident."

"Right, right, confident," she responds, her voice trailing off.

"Okay so what about me? What's wrong with me?"

"There's nothing," the girl says. "There's nothing wrong with your personality."

"You recently bought that computer, no?" my mom says when I arrive at their house for dinner.

"Yeah," I admit.

She shakes her head. She's unfolding a sari she ordered on eBay; draping its raw silk weight over her forearm. UPS delivered it with unexpected duty charges that were more than double what she already paid the seller, defeating the whole purpose of buying a sari on the internet.

"That must be Nina's wedding sari!" says my dad, limping into the room, clutching his piriformis.

"Ayyo, such a cheap sari, no way," says my mom. "And you must be dreaming." She looks at me. "This one is never going to get married."

"Chee, don't say that. Knock on wood," my dad says. He sits at the kitchen table with me, grabs a handful of crispy chickpeas from a bowl on the table, and starts crunching. "How is the dating going?"

The reason I'm online dating is that I'm thirty-one and have never been in a serious relationship. I have Indian parents, who exist to bear children who get married and bear children who get married and bear children, and so on until nuclear war renders us barren. "How can your dad be happy when his only daughter isn't settled?" my mother asks me, on a semi-weekly basis.

"The dating would be going well, except that my laptop was stolen so I never finished my profile," I respond.

"What? Oh jeez," says my dad. "Did you tell the police?"

"Police won't do anything," says my mom, re-folding the sari and tucking it back into its brown paper. "Nirmala Aunty's bicycle was stolen and nothing happened. Now she walks to the office."

"If you need, you can borrow one of our computers," says my dad. "We have too many."

After dinner, he brings me down to the basement where he keeps all his electronics. Against an unfinished concrete wall, he has a row of off-brand Billy bookcases (he's boycotting IKEA because he disapproves of the store layout). The shelves are a thicket of wires—unused USB cables wind around abandoned laptops and nearly every defunct generation of Black-Berry, a brand he continues to buy out of loyalty to Canadian businesses. A VHS player reigns from the top shelf, next to a stack of 5-inch floppy disks. There's also a disassembled Christmas tree on the shelf for no good reason. My dad digs until he finds an adequate laptop—the sound is broken, but it can access internet, and that's all I really need.

Though my profile consists only of a photo where I'm about to be eaten by a shark, my inbox has seven messages. "Hey there beautiful," "how's it going?" "great smile, let's chat," etc. Only one has commented on the shark: "nice Photoshop skills." I delete all the messages except the last. I scan the guy's details: He's 6'1", of mixed European descent, has a job (though it doesn't say what he does), and likes baseball, Indian food and snorkelling. I type back, "Thanks! Have you seen anything interesting in Halifax waters?" My online messaging style is falsely jovial.

I exit his profile and check off a bunch of search filters: single, monogamous, looking for a relationship, employed, speaks English, age thirty to forty. That seems like the bare minimum. What comes up is a catalogue that's unsettlingly infinite—I click through pages of results with no indication of how many pages of results there are. You could scroll on forever. Results appear in a different order if you refresh the page. Do the results repeat? The site's unintuitive interface includes a section that works like Tinder—their biggest competitor—for those who'd rather just swipe through photos. I swipe left on three and then regret it. It's unclear: If you swipe left, will you ever see that person again?

A week later, I'm back at Uncommon Grounds to meet the snorkeller. I arrive early to avoid the awkward shuffle of bill paying. Instead of my usual scone or coffee I'm drinking a cup of genmaicha, to seem like somebody cultured and hydrated with perpetually fresh breath. I had a job interview here a few weeks ago, and the feeling is the same—generalized anxiety. I choose my usual table far back near the window, which was shattered and repaired so recently there's still a small pile of crushed glass swept into one corner. I have a full view of the café so I can see the guy enter. He looks to the right, where there are displays of fancy chocolate bars, packaged rum cake, and sweatshirts screen-printed with Halifax word collages. He looks to the left and I smile. When I stand to greet him I realize that 6'1" is much taller than I thought, or maybe it just seems that way because he's so skinny. I imagine him hovering in a shallow bay, wearing a mask and spitting water. We're a complete physical mismatch—he's about half as wide and twice as tall as me—and I can see in his face that he knows it, too, unless of course I'm "mind misreading," a phenomenon my therapist told me about where you incorrectly assume people are judging you, when they're just thinking about baseball stats or the rare variety of trout they spotted yesterday.

"Hey!" I say.

"Hey." He looks around as though he's trying to find somebody better to talk to. He squints at my face as though he expected a clearer complexion. "You got your own drink?" he asks, pointing at my tea.

"I was just early, so..."

"I would've gotten your drink, but okay," he says. "What's good here? You want anything else?"

"Oh no, I'm okay," I say. "The scones are massive. Also the granola bars use marshmallows as the glue, you know to bind the granola together?"

"That seems fattening," he says. He gestures toward the coffee counter. "I'm going to grab something."

"Oh, sure, go for it."

He leaves and comes back with peppermint tea. "Those scones are far too large. Can you eat a whole one of those? I bet you can't, you're so tiny. Like a bird!" He reaches out and grasps my wrist between his thumb and index finger.

"Oh, no, I usually just eat three bites and save the rest of it," I lie. I'm not so much tiny as average-sized, but I can tell he likes the idea of a woman with bird bones, to tuck into a napkin and pocket like leftover pastry. "I'm more of a tea drinker," I lie. How do I fall in love with somebody who prefers hot toothpaste water to marshmallows? Maybe he's a vegan. Maybe he's an empath who believes he can feel the pain of butchered animals. Maybe he had a heart attack at a tender age. Maybe I will give up butter for him. "Are you a vegan?"

"No, I just don't eat garbage," he says, laughing, and removing the tea bag so it doesn't over-steep. He places the used bag on his napkin, and it leaks onto the table's dark wood grain.

"Have you been here before?" I ask.

"Yep." He sips his tea, bored at my question, or thinking of baseball and trout.

"I come here a lot. I like to do work here 'cause I just can't seem to get anything done at home . . . too many distractions . . . you know like I'll just watch *The Bachelor* when I'm supposed to be working. . ." I'm saying nothing in a lot of words.

He doesn't respond. He sips his tea.

"Actually my laptop was stolen here just a few days ago."

"That sucks," he says. There's a long pause. We both look around as though the walls are of great interest. They're painted to look like vintage signs, weathered text in once-bold colours. "Oh, so that shark photo."

"Yeah?"

"How long ago was that taken?"

"Um, like a month or two, I think?" I know exactly when it was. It was taken the day I quit teaching. I'd had this feeling of sheer freedom, but the stranger taking the photo had waited too long, and the feeling, with my smile, had faltered.

"It doesn't look like you."

I don't know what to say to this, because the photo does look like me, or at least, what I think I look like. But who knows how accurate that is?

"Also, why did you add a shark to the photo?"

"It's a metaphor," I say. "Because doesn't every photo secretly have a shark in it?" Because it's hilarious, dumbass.

He sips his tea.

"And the smile—it doesn't look natural."

"Wait, the shark's smile?" I say.

"No, yours. It's unnatural. You're just smiling for the camera."

"Isn't that what you're supposed to do?"

We talk briefly about snorkelling and Indian food. He explains that it's unlikely a shark would appear in the Halifax harbour. He tells me what the best Indian restaurant in Halifax is. He finishes his tea. We don't hug or mention meeting again. Date over.

I buy a scone and pull out my borrowed laptop to finish some admin work. Though my stolen computer contained all my documents for job applications, I previously installed online backup, so I can access my documents online. I download what I need, but as I'm searching through the folders, I notice a file I don't recognize: me.bmp. Curious, I download that, too. I don't know what I thought it would be, but it opens in Microsoft Paint and shows a photo of a girl around thirteen years old. She's mid-strut, dark-haired, brown-skinned, fish-cheeked like a model, but from her eyes you can tell she's hamming for the camera. She stands in an orange-toned living room. She's utterly confident. I wonder who took the photo, and imagine a friend the same age, the two of them in that limbo time between school and dinner. Around the image, she's used the paintbrush tool to draw sloppy stars in white and red.

When I go home I change into sweatpants and the T-shirt I got at Two If By Sea, a Dartmouth café where the croissants are the size of a healthy baby. The shirt says, EAT MORE BUTTER. I sit alone in bed smoking a bowl and watching *The Bachelor* with no sound and eating cake with my hands, wishing aliens would abduct me so I wouldn't have to worry about unromantic things like online dating. I smile with the fakest smile I can muster. Frosting in my teeth. As the Bachelor does damage control on a group date, I reflect on the dating website's competing interests: Yes, they want users to find love on the site for positive word-of-mouth and so they can post people's photos and quotes on the Success Stories page, but it's also in their interest to keep relationships failing, to keep you coming back. We are each Sisyphus; instead of pushing a rock we click a touchpad button. Instead of getting exercise we atrophy in our desk chairs and develop carpal tunnel. Or maybe we're that guy whose liver is repeatedly eaten by vultures (I should know his name, since I taught my Grade nines about him in the mythology unit), but instead we corrode our organs with bottomless cups of coffee and pints of Rickard's Red. Online dating is an embarrassing punishment for a mediocre crime: not finding love in the pre-internet world.

My stolen laptop backs up twice a week, so I start checking on Mondays and Thursdays. On Monday there's another photo—a selfie this time, of the same girl with a shimmery face and eyelashes so long and so false they make the photo look 3D. "Makeover!" she's scrawled with the Microsoft paintbrush. I want to teach her how to use Photoshop. I want to Photoshop a shark into the background with a speech bubble and send it to her. *Give me my laptop, or else.* The next Monday there's a crudely assembled meme—a Shiba Inu with a knowing look. He's been cropped and pasted on a loaf of bread, topped with broken English phrases in Comic Sans (*wow—so hip—much happy*). Thursday there's a pair of tanned, thigh-gapped legs on a beach, though it might only be a pair of glistening hot dogs set next to each other to look like legs. It's the newest meme—hot dog legs. On Monday there's Grumpy Cat, grumping about Mondays.

Mystery: Is this meme-loving girl the laptop thief? Was it planned? Did she lurk in the Uncommon Grounds waiting for a trusting dimwit to use the bathroom? Did she eat anything while she was there? Did she place a decoy mug in front of her? Did she merely buy the laptop from an amateur thief without the knowledge to reformat a computer?

There is no name on the photos; no identifying detail. But if I'm patient, I figure she'll eventually upload a homework assignment with a name on it, and then I'll call the police. Unless she's the type of student who always forgets to include her name.

On Date #2, not an online date but one set up by my mother, I tell the guy I used to be a teacher. He says, "Teaching is a good job for a woman." He says, "Just so we're clear, if this works out, you'll move to my house in Moncton and get a job within a practical driving distance."

When my mom calls to see how the date went, I tell her what the guy said, and she says, "Teaching *is* a good job for a woman." She reminds me that Moncton has dinner theatre and a mini indoor amusement park. "Give him a chance," she says. "How can your dad be happy when his only daughter is unsettled?"

Date #3 is with a doctor. We go for a glass of wine at Obladee, a local wine bar, since coffee dates might as well be job interviews, except if you get the job you must marry the interviewer and have sex with him for the rest of your life. He has red hair and sunburned arms. Shouldn't doctors know about sunscreen?

"Another glass?" he asks after I've savoured my Nova 7— tart, coral pink, and delicately sparkling. I sample it every week at the Halifax Seaport Market, pretending I've never had it before. I consider a second glass, but I haven't eaten, so I suggest a walk instead. He doesn't like this. "Or how about mini-golf?" he asks. His smile looks like he's pretending.

"I didn't know we had mini-golf in downtown Halifax," I say.

"Oh, it's just outside of town. I have my car, so we can drive there." He smiles again, showing his pointy incisors, which seem like an obvious sign that I should not get in his car.

"Could we do that next time maybe? I'd still be up for a walk though, like just around the waterfront? We could get ice cream at COWS…"

He gets the check. We go for a walk. We sit on a bench facing the water. He puts a hand on my knee. An unleashed dog approaches. It's a black lab holding a stick between its teeth. I see its owner way down the boardwalk. I scratch the dog's ears and his tail wags.

The dog points his nose at the doctor. "Nice doggie," says the doctor. He doesn't touch the dog. "What do you want, doggie?" His voice is as flat as Saskatchewan.

Obviously the dog wants somebody to throw the stick, so I throw the stick. The dog bounds away. I wish I was a flea buried in his fur, so I could go too.

"Well, how about I give you a ride home?" says the doctor.

"Oh, that's okay, I live really close." Not true.

"It's late, though. You'll be cold."

"No, no, I need the exercise. I have a sweater."

"My car is parked right over there." He points at an expensive black vehicle in an empty lot.

"I'm literally five minutes from here."

"Okay," he says.

We stand up. He holds his arms out for a hug, so we hug. He clutches my shoulders and his hands feel like talons. He kisses me on the mouth, uninvited, off-centre, hard-lipped.

The next day I get a text. *I'm barbecuing, want to come over? I could come pick you up?*

I Google for polite ways to decline a second date. I text: *Hey, it was really great chatting with you yesterday. I don't think we're quite a match, but I wish you luck on your search!*

No response. I will never know what kind of doctor he was. Pathologist? I search *The Coast* for news of murders.

On Date #4 I'm asked: Why are you still single? It's not the first time I've been asked this question. *How has nobody snatched you up?* "I'm selective," I say.

This might be the truth. In university I dumped a guy after two months because he wouldn't watch an Alfred Hitchcock movie, not because he was afraid, but because it was in black and white. "You'll regret this," he said. "I've dated girls way prettier than you."

Another had a running gag about molding the perfect girlfriend—"If I could mold the perfect girlfriend. . ." he'd say, and then list the qualities of mine he wanted to change—the length of my hair, the courses I'd signed up for, the amount of time I spent talking about baked goods.

Another, late at night after a party, while walking me back to my dorm room, pointed at a bush and said, "That would be a good place to rape a girl."

Another I dumped because he always rubbed his fingers together when talking about money, as though he couldn't contain the itch of wanting to have it, and later when he shoved his fingers inside me it seemed so greedy; I knew he would take whatever he could.

If this were a horror movie, each Monday or Thursday I'd check my online backup and find something worse: An animated GIF of a screaming mouth. A suicide note with no signature. A JPEG of the inside of my apartment, a shark pasted into it. Found footage of a violent death.

Instead on Monday there's only a video of a preteen girl dancing. She wears a pale-yellow leotard and a grey hoodie. She dances with bare feet on shag carpet. I drag and drop a screenshot of her into Google Image Search. I find only pictures of other girls in yellow leotards, who otherwise look nothing like her. I go back to the video. She's in a basement, I think. The room is dark and golden. She wheels her arms, touches her toes, eyes shut. The leotard creases at her flat waist. Due to the laptop's missing sound card, I can't hear the music. I imagine the soft tick of high-hat. I feel the song's beat through each snap of movement, each bent limb.

Five weeks after my laptop is stolen, the girl uploads a selfie with a name signed at the bottom. *Teena*, it says. I type the name into Twitter, Facebook, then Instagram, and I find her—she's posted the same selfie in her Instagram account. Teena Mitchell—the only Teena (spelled that way) in Halifax. Her Instagram also has a photo of her in the modest lawn out front of a row house. I call the police at their non-emergency number. "I don't know where the house is exactly, but I know she's in the metro area, I have her name, and I have a photo of her," I say.

"Who is this, Nancy Drew?" asks the man on the phone. He laughs and laughs.

But a couple of days later I get a phone call from a police officer who says he's downstairs and has my laptop. I buzz him up. "Here it is!" he hands it to me. "Great detective work."

"How did you find the house?" I ask.

"Oh, we recognized it right away. It's part of an affordable housing project down on Gottingen. I went over there and the kid just started crying, 'It wasn't me! I'm innocent!'"

In my hands, the laptop feels heavy and unfamiliar. I turn it around. There's a bright sticker over the Dell logo. *Just dance dance dance,* it says.

I meet Date #5 at Uncommon Grounds. It's safer here. It's walking distance. There's no alcohol except in the rum cake. The only thieves are little girls.

He buys a bar of dark chocolate with bits of pistachio and dried apricot, unwraps it delicately, like he's Charlie searching for a golden ticket. He places the chocolate on top of the wrapper, on the table between us, and motions for me to share. "I like this place," he says. "Good food and sweatshirt options."

"It's a great place," I say. "The scones are massive."

"Massive scones—amazing!"

We're quiet for a moment, but I feel okay. A square of chocolate melts against my palate, and I can see that he's mulling over what to say next.

"So, you said on your profile that you *used to* be a teacher. Can I ask why you don't teach anymore? If it's not too personal..."

"Oh no, that's okay. I guess I just wasn't ... you have so much influence as a teacher. Over children's lives." I've surprised myself by being honest. Usually if the topic comes up, I say the marking and lesson prep were cutting into my me-time. "Maybe that makes me sound like a coward."

"Not at all," he says, "I get that. No judgment, I spend most of my day hiding behind a screen."

"Speaking of screens, my laptop was stolen here a month or two ago."

"Oh shit, not your laptop," he says. "You must be a loyal customer, though, to keep coming here."

"I did manage to get the laptop back." I tell him what happened. I tell it like it's a funny story. "The police called me Nancy Drew."

"But wait, what happened to the girl?"

"I don't know," I say. I don't tell him that what will happen to her is what happens to every girl. That her experiences will empty her. That there's a point when a girl becomes a meme, a facsimile transmitted, a carbon copy folded and passed along. That she'll end up a weak and staticky version of the original. I don't tell him I can't stop thinking about her, or that they never asked me about pressing charges—is that only an option you're given on TV? I don't know what the consequences are.

I tell him about the table we're sitting at—my usual table by the repaired window. I was here when the window broke. A deer came crashing through the glass, then thrashed for five minutes, leaping onto tables, trying to get out. Customers held up chairs as shields, protecting themselves and each other. We huddled by the bathroom hallway. We clutched each other for safety, in a cloud of coffee breath. They found the deer later, confused and injured, with deep lacerations on its back and belly. In the CBC article about the incident, a quote from a witness: "I don't know how it didn't get its blood on us."

I go on four more dates with this guy. He's the kindest person I've ever met. He wants to lock it down. "We should go to the food truck festival," he says, though the food truck fest is two months away, and we have committed nothing to each other. He holds my hand and tells me he wants me to meet his friends. He asks permission before he kisses me. He tells me he's deactivated his dating account. When I sign in, his photo has been replaced by a faint grey outline of a man. "I'm not interested in meeting anybody else," he says. I deactivate my account, too. I picture marrying him, under strands of twinkle lights and white mayflowers on the roof of the Seaport Market. I know my parents would like him. But I put off answering his next message. It goes unanswered, and so does the next. I ghost him. I'm a ghost.

The next time I check, Teena's Instagram account is gone.

What I imagine is this: She's walking home from a summer job babysitting for a family in the South End. Headphones on, she's shimmying slightly as she walks, thinking about dancing, about the shape and positioning of her feet—heel, arch, toe. She wants to record herself, so she can play it back and perfect her movements, but she doesn't own a recording device. It's a long distance from here to Gottingen, so she stops at Uncommon Grounds for a $3 treat—hot chocolate, or a granola bar made with marshmallows. She sees an unguarded laptop on a table, slides her headphones down and glances around quickly, then slips it into her backpack and walks away without looking behind her. Her heart is beating fast. She'll never come to this café again. Ahead of her are the laptop's limitless possibilities—and the future, opening up like a mouth.

GOOD MEDICINE

Megan Callahan

My therapist asks me to give my anxiety form, so I turn it into a beast.

Most of the time he's wolf-like, grey and lean, with wet jaws that bite at my heels. Every morning as I twist open the blinds, the beast stands in the early light and howls. He circles me as I steep tea, as I pick at my milk-soggy cornflakes. Sometimes I shout and sling my spoon at his maw, but he always leaps out of the way, letting it ping and slide across the ceramic tiles. He flicks his tail, and when he snarls it's almost a laugh. If he gets too close, his fur stings like nettles. His breath smells of mulch and decomposing earth. Eventually, I give in. I let him stalk my shadow. When I walk down the street, I hear the click-clack of his claws. At the café, he roves between round oak tables, sniffing the legs of oblivious customers, and his glass eyes watch me press grinds into the portafilter. Even when I'm at school in the cavernous lecture hall, the heavy doors shut and my professor's voice booming up from the podium, I can hear him just outside. Scraping at the threshold.

*

"Come to my yoga class," Hélène says as she rolls out the mop bucket brimming with bleach water. Her French accent distorts the vowels so it sounds like she's saying *yug-ah*. "It will unblock your flow." She makes a wave motion with her hands like she's a hula dancer on a beach, her tangled hair dark and swaying down her back.

"Maybe." I shoot her a smile from across the half-moon counter. She shrugs. This is what I always say.

On weekends, Hélène and I share the night shift. From ten to eleven, girls in red stilettos and body-form dresses toss back shots of espresso before teetering to the clubs on St-Laurent and St-Denis. Homeless men with plastic bags in their shoes shuffle in to sleep and smoke in the back alcove, drowning cigarette butts in half-empty cups of dark roast. It's almost midnight now, closing time, and Hélène's mixed CD blasts "Creep" into the empty café. She sings along and sloshes the mop's grey tendrils through ash and boot grime while I stack the clean porcelain, dump coffee grounds in the trash.

Hélène has anxiety, too. She talks about chakras, practises yoga five times a week, and crowds her Little Italy apartment with tropical, leafy vines. She believes in the cleansing power of burnt sage and crystals, and every so often has a meltdown in the stockroom.

I tell her I might switch majors. I show her my class notebooks, lined pages filled with nothing but caricatures of my hook-nosed English professor. "I hate Shakespeare," I say. "If I have to read one more sonnet, I'm going to hurl."

Hélène thinks I'm crazy. Her dream is to move to the South of France and write books of erotic poetry. Every few months, she tells me she's going back to school. "I'm ready," she says. "*J'te jure*, this time I'm ready." If I were to give Hélène's anxiety form, it would be a python: wrapped around her ribcage, holding her in place, scales rippling like water as the muscles underneath squeeze and release, squeeze and release.

*

I arrive at the walk-in clinic before 8 a.m., but there's already half a dozen people in line. When a nurse unlocks the door, we shamble inside like doomed cattle. The waiting room smells like hand sanitizer and despair. I collapse in a plastic chair and bounce my knee, listening to the steady patter of sick-person complaints. The beast prowls nearby. I cover myself with my coat and try to melt into the goose down folds. Time slugs forward. Eventually, a woman's voice calls out my name. "Door two," she says.

I drag myself down the hall. Behind the white door is another white room. An examination table is spread with crinkly paper. A nurse swings open the far door, holding a clipboard. She's almost pretty. Bumps of acne beneath too-thick makeup. Irises that seep from green to gold.

The nurse speaks in staccatos. Age, profession, symptoms, history? I'm breathless and stuttering. She takes a flurry of notes before slipping out the door. As it swings, I glimpse the beast's glistening white teeth.

I'm pacing by the time the doctor strides in. He's wearing bright yellow runners. Grey wisps of hair tuft above his ears. "Good morning, Claire!" He shakes my hand like I've just won an amazing prize. He gives me his name, which I promptly forget. I'm distracted by his shoes, their splash of freshly squeezed lemon yellow, the only colour in the room.

"Let's start with a little questionnaire." From a drawer he pulls out a form: *The Wellbeing Screening*. My fingers find a pen, and I can hear the beast snarl with every box that I tick. "Sorry," I say, and the doctor doesn't ask why I'm crying, just hands me a tissue box and whistles some tuneless song. I blow my nose as he scrawls a prescription.

"Think of it as medicine," he says cheerfully. "Like antibiotics for an infection." He guffaws like this is the funniest thing he's ever said. "We'll start you on two every morning. Come back in three months."

Downstairs, the pharmacist slides a plastic pill bottle across the counter. The beast brushes against my joggers. "You might experience side effects," the man says as he hands me a pamphlet. I cram it into my coat pocket and dump out my crumpled fives, only half listening. The pills, flat and pink like Pez candy, cost less than a thirty-minute therapy session. I feel them rattle in my bag as I walk out the door.

At sunrise the next morning, I swallow two with my tea. The beast watches from the doorway. Slinks across the floor.

*

"Medication can be helpful," my therapist says. "To silence those alarm bells." She taps her temple with a ruby-red fingernail. Her blonde hair shimmers in an iron-flat bob. There's a tiny rip in my jeans and I stick my finger in it, start to tear at the threads. My therapist's office is all blues and greens. There are plants on the shelves and coloured markers on the coffee table. She keeps pads of white paper tucked in a drawer. Sometimes, she takes them out and asks me to draw spirals.

"It's an exercise to quiet my mind," she says.

I wonder what she does with them after, if she has a fat yellow folder somewhere filled with hundreds of my colourful seashell whorls.

She asks me where the beast is today. "Here," I say. I'm crying again and this makes me angry. My therapist nods, serene. "You've been feeding him," she says.

"I have to. If I don't, he'll eat me."

She clucks her tongue, laces her fingers across her ample chest.

"If you keep feeding him, he'll never leave."

As if hearing his name, the beast looks up from the carpeted floor. His eyes gleam.

"There are some things we can try," she says, "to break the habit."

I nod. Already I've decided to cancel my next session.

The wind snaps my scarf straight as I step out into the dark. The beast lopes behind. It is Day Two of my medication. As I walk to the metro, I imagine the pills dissolving in my gut, seeping into my bloodstream and scattering like dust.

*

Day Fifteen. The beast is missing.

It happens like that, from one day to the next. No big fanfare, no fireworks. At the café I feel weightless, like an untethered balloon. I almost skip behind the counter as I restock the shelves. I smile till my cheeks ache at the winter-weary customers.

"No side effects?" Hélène asks. She's foaming milk for her signature cinnamon latte.

"Only nausea," I say. A half lie.

"*Incroyable!* We need to celebrate."

At midnight, we lock up and tramp through deep snow.

Inside the pub, the crowd is thick and sweaty. Conversations are hectic. I grab a table near the door and Hélène brings us two dewy pints. As I sip mine, she slaps her pack of tarot cards on the table and asks me to shuffle. She winks and laughs as I roll my eyes. Hélène loves reading me. After I cut the deck, she begins the ten-card spread, then flips them over one by one. My eyes linger on the Lovers reversed before travelling to the red-haired Queen of Swords. My favourite card.

"Interesting," Hélène says. "This is very positive." Her ringed fingers fly around the table as she breaks down my past and present, paints vague pictures of my future.

In the back of my mind, I'm waiting for the beast to howl.

Hélène is flirting with the curvy waitress at the bar when a man touches my shoulder. He leans in to be heard through the thicket of noise. His suit screams *business student*. His hair is neatly parted.

He brings me a glass of Scotch. It's good Scotch, I can tell. Dark and expensive. It tastes syrupy and cloying, but I swallow it anyway. His name is Daniel, he says. He talks, I listen. It's the

sound of his voice, mostly, that I like. He tells me he's intern-
ing at his father's company, that he plays tenor saxophone and
likes free jazz. He asks about my tattoos and touches them one
by one. His jokes are predictable and goofish but I laugh anyway, brush my knee against his. He buys me another Scotch.

We're both drunk when we get back to my apartment. He
tugs off my jeans, pulls off my wet socks. He's serious now,
focused. Clumsy hands unbutton my sweater. "God, you're
hot," he says. I giggle and cover my eyes. Fuck, I think. I'm so
drunk. He's kissing my neck and I wait for my body to warm,
to open. His hungry mouth travels across my skin, his tongue
slips inside me but I'm so cold. "Do you like this?" he says. I tell
him I'm tired. I blame the Scotch. Afterwards, I lie awake in
the dark and listen to his snores. Watch the headlights of passing cars flood my window and vanish.

*

Day Thirty-Five. Woolly snow piles on my balcony and down
the corkscrew staircase. I leave footprints in it, crunch through
the pristine white. The world is muted and colourless. In the
bus shelter, I pull out the pharmacist's rumpled pamphlet and
read the section on side effects for the millionth time. I've jot-
ted notes in the margins. Circled words with a red pen.

I think I've lost weight. Eating has become tiresome. I live
off cereal and tea, the occasional can of soup. Daniel cooks
real meals, pasta with Bolognese sauce and Duck à l'Orange.
For breakfast, he fries eggs in his stainless-steel pan and I
hover over the stovetop, waiting for the smell to send signals
to my brain. What is hunger, I think. What is fullness? He says
I eat like a bird and laughs at my small bites. I haven't told him
about the pills.

Daniel's twelfth-floor condo is a study in beige. Fish tank
windows overlook a glittering downtown, send shocks of ver-
tigo up my spine. In the morning, he makes his bed military
style, with ClingWrap corners and diagonal folds. He says my

Mile End one-bedroom is charming, uses the word *quirky*. Every piece of furniture was scavenged from thrift stores and my parent's suburban split-level. I leave my dirty underwear dangling from doorknobs, forget paperbacks between couch cushions and on top of the microwave. When Daniel comes over, he bristles like a cat. He tidies compulsively, determined to instill order. I don't discourage him.

Sometimes, we sleep together. Inside I feel nothing, as if my body is wrapped in gauze. I think about what my therapist said about alarm bells and wonder if mine are still going off, somewhere in the dark sub-basement of my mind, but I just can't hear them.

*

Day Sixty-Two. Snow pelts my bedroom window. School cancelled, the radio crackles. All stores closed. It's still early. Pearly light leaks in between the slats of blinds, and I hear the distant groan of the plow on a nearby street, its shrill and looping siren disturbing the silence.

I sit in bed and consider the pills on my nightstand. Their nauseating pink. Yesterday, the pharmacist handed me my third refill. Thirty more days, he said, as I laid out my tip money. The cap's seal is unbroken.

Slowly, like in a dream, I slide open my underwear drawer. Bury the bottle in the back, beneath my balled-up wool socks. Something inside me unhooks and releases. I pad barefoot into the kitchen. Fill the kettle with water.

*

As soon as I open my eyes, I can tell something's different.

I hear water running, Daniel whistling in the shower. My room is dark and cold. The electric baseboard heater smells of burnt dust. I crawl out of bed and twist open the blinds. Blink in the sudden glare.

The howl.

53

My insides shrivel up.

"Fuck," I say. "You again."

I turn. The beast has grown. Like a wild thing from that book my dad read to me as a child, he's standing on his hind legs and showing me his fangs. His once-grey fur now charcoal black. Drool trickles down his chin and when he opens his jaws, the guttural voice that comes out is almost human.

I sink to the floor.

"What's wrong?" Daniel is dripping in the doorway, a towel slung around his waist.

"I can't go to class."

"Are you sick?"

Yes, I want to say. I'm sick, sick in the head. There's a monster in my room and he's trying to fucking eat me.

Instead I start crying, wet and hacking sobs that tear at my throat. Daniel crouches and pats me lightly on the arm. His wetness gives me goosebumps.

"Maybe the flu," he tries.

I haul myself back into bed and pull the comforter up. I watch him button his shirt and slick back his hair. He leaves a bowl next to the bed and twists the blinds shut.

"Call me when you're feeling better," he says. He kisses me on the head before walking out the door. I know that I won't.

*

I call in sick to work for the next three days. My phone buzzes but I ignore it. I make tea and I sleep. I take baths when I get cold. The water is too hot but I sink into the tub anyway. I lay in the dark. Door locked, submerged to my nose. I keep my head underwater for as long as possible, only coming up for air when my lungs threaten to burst. Outside the beast snarls, but the water keeps him muffled. There is only my heartbeat. Only the occasional whoosh of my breath.

*

I'm crying again. I'd forgotten what it was like to cry so much that your eyelids blow up like balloons, stay swollen for days. "It's the salt," Hélène said, when I finally let her in the apartment. "Gives you froggy eyes."

She booked this appointment for me, scrolling through my contacts as I pawed at her from the bed and whispered meek protests. Now I'm curled on my therapist's office couch, a nest of wadded tissues piled on my lap.

"Crying is healthy," my therapist says. "You're eliminating toxins." She swivels in her chair and taps her nails on the armrest. This time they're turquoise, like the sea. "Where is the beast today?"

"Here."

The beast is sitting next to me. Inches away. Silent now, and smaller than he was. But his fur is still black, and his teeth are still fangs. I shudder when he moves. Dig my nails into my palms.

"He's not trying to eat you, Claire."

"Bullshit."

She pauses. The clock on the wall ticks loud and maddening. Finally, she leans forward and pulls a fresh pad of paper from the coffee table drawer.

"Let's try something new," she says.

*

Dusk after an April rain. From the balcony, the air smells of ice melting into thawing earth, of lime-green buds emerging from sleep. The beast is beside me, nose in the wind. The mug in my hands is warm and steaming. Before leaving for her hatha class, Hélène brewed a pot of honey-sweetened stinging nettle. This month she's given up caffeine and drinks only herbal teas and infusions. Boxes of rooibos and ginseng fill her little cabinets, and calendulas are sprouting in an egg carton on her windowsill. I call Hélène my healer, and this makes her laugh.

My new medication is round and white. Each pill is scored with a hairline groove. "To make splitting easier," the doctor said, "when we lower your dose." I smiled and plucked the new prescription from his hand, but secretly hated his casual use of *when*, as if he knew something I didn't. As if my future could be read.

Above rooftops, pink and mauve cirrus clouds spread like threaded cotton candy. The beast is up and hungry, restless and pacing across the wrought-iron balcony. Later, when the sky turns deep indigo, I'll lace up my running shoes and go out into the chilly night. I'll run down my street, past my neighbours' curtained windows, and into the lamp-lit park, where the trail winds under maples and circles the shallow pond. When I run, the beast always lopes close behind. Panting and snapping, his claws scraping the gravel path. But sometimes, if the wind is right, I see him change. His pointed ears start to round and droop. His prickly fur turns soft and brown. And if I run for long enough, fast enough and far enough, even his howl starts to sound different. Less like a wolf. More like the bark of a dog I once loved.

ASLEEP TILL YOU'RE AWAKE

Francine Cunningham

My dead mom was sitting in the waiting room at the walk-in clinic. I was there because I'd been falling asleep in weird places. The first time happened in a grocery store. I was holding two boxes of cereal and I got tired so I sat down in the aisle. I never used to just sit in grocery stores but when you get that tired you have no choice. When your eyes are burning and the blinks are coming slower and slower it becomes impossible not to sit. So I sat. And then I leaned. I should never have leaned. I should have sat straight like someone who does yoga but I don't do yoga. I don't even stretch, really.

So, I was sitting, then leaning, and then a man with a brown coat and black sneakers was shaking my shoulder asking me if I was dead. Okay, he was asking if I was fine but basically that's the same thing. So, he asked me if I was fine and I said no. And then he just walked away. Like who does that? I said no, you're supposed to help, but he walked away and I got up. I didn't even buy any cereal. I just went home. And the days kept happening like that. Being shaken awake by strangers with glasses, or lumpy sweaters, or stinky breath, or frizzy hair, or dry patches of skin. It was annoying.

So, I went to the doctor. I sat in the office for like forever and then she was shaking my shoulder, the doctor, waking me up. I mumbled an apology that I didn't mean. How many of those do you think we do in a year, apologies we don't mean? I must do a hundred. Or maybe more, maybe more than 300 hundred even. I don't know. I should track it like a food diary addict tracks calories. But I know I won't.

This doctor, she was all in my face asking me questions, like I just got up lady, give me a second to breathe. But you know how it is in those offices, they're like little rats scurrying from one beige office to the next, five minutes staring into the desperate eyes of a person wanting to feel better from a cold that's caused by a virus and knowing there is nothing they can do. Like have you never seen a bus ad before person? Fluids and rest stupid. No, rich people don't take the bus. They never see the ads us poor people do. Oh, I should mention I didn't go to the walk-in clinic by my house. No, I went into the neighbourhood with houses that were all the same house, not ones that were sectioned off into many different apartments and suites like mine. Overflowing with kids learning to play the trumpet and clothing on balconies. I decided that for this sleeping thing I needed a real big shot doctor. But guess what? This doctor had the same dead-eyed look that the ones near my house did. Like they were staring at you and thinking about roasting a chicken for dinner.

Anyway, she told me to go to a place to get my blood drawn, that it was probably nothing. That I was overreacting. But she would order the blood test anyway because it couldn't hurt. And I thought she only did that because maybe she made extra money if she sent people to this place to get blood drawn. That maybe she only got paid if she did something other than say two sentences in the small office with one window and a hard bed covered in tissue paper. But I don't know. I never went to the blood drawing place. I don't like needles.

When I came out of the doctor's office I saw her. My mom. No, I should say my dead mom. She was sitting in a chair reading a magazine. A boring magazine, too. One she would never have read when she was alive. One about gardening. Or at least it had a flower on the cover. But she was reading it anyhow and she had her legs crossed just like I remembered her always sitting, one foot caught behind her calf, her toe keeping everything in place. Her hair was the same. A short burgundy dyed bob cut on an angle up her jaw. The little tiny hairs on my neck stood up. I was seeing a ghost and no one cared. Moved even. I wanted to say something. Like a lot I did, but instead I started to laugh. It was this belly laugh kind of thing. It spewed out of me and all over the waiting room. But she didn't even look up. My dead mom. She just kept reading her magazine about rotting plants and diseases that bugs trample all over your hard work. And I kept laughing through the cracks in my teeth.

She was wearing the same sandals and shorts I remember seeing her in on the day she walked away from me for the last time. We were in another place, a town, a dusty kind of beat-up houses and scraggly brown grass with garbage just thrown out of windows and dogs roaming free kind of place. She was living there then. With her fiancé what's-his-name. And I went to visit because I needed to leave the sounds of the city hitting my brain all the time. But I could tell that he didn't want me there. He had already claimed my dead mom as his own. He even put a gross tarnished brass ring on her finger. The skin under it was this sickly green that leeched into her. Her once-blue eyes turning from something found under clear ocean water to this muddy stagnant moss-covered body of water instead. He was like an infection that can't be treated with antibiotics. Sores oozing white pus. I stayed because I knew he wanted me gone.

But I couldn't not fight with him. Or her by the end. I don't even know why. I just couldn't hold the words in. I tried.

Really, I did, but when someone is just so wrong about everything you have to say something, right? And when not saying something makes your teeth clench so hard and for so long that the front ones start to wiggle free and are in constant pain, so much so that you can only consume liquid dinners, well you have to let the words burst free. So I did. And then my mom started to hate me. I think. But I don't really know.

They took me to the bus stop. Just dropped me off like an unwanted couch infested with moths. But I couldn't stop saying things. So, we yelled until we were hoarse and when she walked away from me I tried to yell that I still loved her even though she fell in love with a human pile of garbage, but she didn't hear me because of all the yelling from before. And she didn't turn around. And then I heard on the phone one day last month that she was dead. And I could only think of how if he hadn't been an open sore leaking congealed waste that she would have heard me when I said I loved her. But instead I saw her back walking away, her shorts and sandals, her bob cut too jagged by the neck, a yellow shirt with a stain over the left hip.

After I finished laughing I decided to sit in the chair beside my dead mom. Even though I was finished with the beige room and the not-caring doctor and had to go home to let my cat out of the bathroom where I kept her when I left the house so she didn't pee on my mattress again. I sat right beside her, too. Waited for her to notice me. I breathed her in while I waited. She had this lilac perfume on that I thought smelled gross. Who wants to smell like a dead plant baby? That's what flowers are in a way. The dead plant babies that hang off stems. But she had it slathered on her skin and behind her ears and on her wrists and I breathed it in deep and realized my mom had never smelled like anything other than garlicy BO when she was alive but maybe in death you get to choose perfume from the expensive aisle in the store. I looked at her finger. The green sickness was gone. Her skin was bare. I wanted to vault into the air and scream in glee. She had left human garbage man. She was finally free. But I stayed still. I didn't want a breeze to blow her over and have her melt away. I didn't know the rules of ghosts. I leaned back in the chair as I waited for her look to up.

A nurse with crinkled skin shook me awake. Her face was right in mine. Her hot breath pouring into my nostrils and I recoiled. She was saying something about me needing to leave. They were closing. I reached for my dead mom. But I was alone in the room with crinkle nurse. My heart hammered, like for real, hammered in my chest. It hurt. Where was my mom? Why didn't she wake me up before she left? Why didn't she turn around? Why did she walk away?

I left the doctor's office. But the next day I couldn't stop thinking of her sitting in the chair. I had found her but I had let myself fall asleep. I was stupid. And dumb. And an idiot. I should have reached out to her as soon I saw her. I should have whispered into her ear. I should have said I was sorry. But I didn't. The thoughts were burrowing by then. They had nested in my frontal cortex and they were burrowing and taking over all the other regions of my brain. And I couldn't stop myself from going back once I stepped out of my apartment the next day. I headed straight to the doctor's office. She had to be there, right? What would you have done? Just not gone back? When you knew there was a chance your dead mom would be sitting in a chair waiting for you? But she wasn't. Not the next day, either. Or the next. Or the next. Or infinity of days waiting.

I sit in her chair now when I wait for her. The one she was in when I saw her. And I still smell the flower perfume. Not like a lot. But a little. Like a whiff of something. Like when you're sitting outside in the summer and the breeze carries a hint of rotting garbage and you want to get up and go inside but it's just so nice in the sun so you just smell past it. And when I sit here I imagine following her back to where she came from. There must have been a portal nearby or maybe a gateway to heaven or maybe hell or maybe when my mom died she went to live with the aliens. She always liked talking about aliens. Reading about them, too. And watching You-Tube videos filled with men yelling at the screen about how they were coming to get us. But I don't really know about that. Why would aliens be interested in such a garbage planet filled with such garbage people? I guess maybe they only came for the penguins. I would travel the universe to watch penguins slide around, wouldn't you?

I try not to fall asleep when I sit here waiting for her. I keep my eyes as wide as possible. And I wait for the moment of arrival. Because this time I am going to say something. I am going to say sorry. I am going to tell her I really love her. I am going to ask her to take me with her this time. To live with the aliens. Or in heaven. Or even hell. I don't care.

THROUGH THE COVID-GLASS

Lucia Gagliese

March 12, 2020   **Canada: 1 death/117 cases**

Quarantining alone, as of this afternoon, as of four hours ago when my plane landed, bringing me home to Toronto. I dropped off my suitcase, set up a sanitization centre in the foyer (sanitizer, disinfectant, paper towels), and went to the grocery store. I didn't know it wasn't allowed, that I shouldn't leave my condo, not even for groceries. What if I've spread contagion?

Suitcase unpacked, laundry started, groceries disinfected, bra off, pajamas on. Now what?

Quarantine Daily Plan:

1 Work
   – install telemedicine app
2 Re-watch Cary Grant's filmography
3 Cook/bake
4 Exercise
5 Read
6 Housework
7 Call mom
   – every other day

8 Contact one friend
   – Lori, Patty, Cat, Hatta, Bay
Ready.
Today's movie: *Alice in Wonderland*

Day 3   **1 death/252 cases**

There were no travel adviseries when I left Canada in February, but still I packed disinfectant wipes, disposable gloves, hand sanitizer, surgical masks. I was too self-conscious to wear my mask on the plane, but I did wipe down my seat, seatbelt, table, armrest, window.

"What?" the man next to me scoffed. "You think I have coronavirus?" The woman with him laughed.

"I'm obsessive." I shrugged, not embarrassed exactly, closer to judged, picked-on. But I kept wiping.

Now, I think I understand. Protecting myself implied *he* was dangerous. So, he mocked me to protect *himself*. I keep thinking about him, wondering if he remembers, if he wears a mask, if he's healthy.

Today's movie: *The Talk of the Town*

Day 10   **22 deaths/1469 cases**

Dinah, my realtor and neighbour, died today. Not of COVID, not even suddenly, but after a long illness. She helped me find my condo and then sold it to me, representing both buyer and seller. I didn't mind. I went in under-asking, despite her urging it would never work. It worked.

The home Dinah helped me buy is the home I'd dreamed of living in since I was a girl. From the Don River Valley, I'd look up at this trident-shaped high-rise and wish it was my home. In my first basement apartment, I hung a bird's-eye view of the Don Valley on the wall, wishing it was my view. Dinah made my wishes come true.

COVID has robbed her husband, Bill, of the balms of bereavement: funeral, burial, shared rites, shared tears. But it won't steal my condolences. I write my note, put on my mask, break quarantine, and venture downstairs to Dinah and Bill's condo, Bill's condo now. I disinfect the envelope, lean it against ~~their~~ his door.

Today's movie: *Mr. Blandings Builds His Dream House*

Day 15   66 deaths/4682 cases

Every morning, I read the statistics, but they don't tell the story. Humanity is in the singular. In my colleagues waving silly goodbyes at the end of Zoom meetings. In my patients, healthcare workers themselves, starting sessions with relief at avoiding infection for another week. In Lori texting a video of the Muppets singing *With a Little Help from My Friends*. In my niece hugging herself as a proxy. In Mom, reading page after page of obituaries in the Italian newspapers, seeing her family, her children, herself in each one.

Today's movie: *The Awful Truth*

Day 20   175 deaths/9560 cases

I am being carried by those who went before. Every day, I watch them in their silent films. They move too fast, express too much. Buster Keaton sinks his handmade boat, Charlie Chaplin adopts his foundling, and Harold Lloyd puts his safety last. They are funny, full of life. But it's more than that. In these films from the early 1920s, it's as if the Spanish Flu pandemic never happened, as if their lives were uninterrupted. But they were interrupted. Silent film stars died, moviegoers died, movie production stopped. And yet, only a year or two later, no masks, no contagion, no distancing. No new normal.

Their survival whispers hope.

Day 23   360 deaths/12,978 cases

I share the elevator with Bill. We are masked, standing at diagonal corners, as distanced as possible. I ask how he's doing. He shakes his head, sighs, looks down. When the elevator stops at his floor, he asks me to wait. He hurries along the dim hallway. His door opens, closes, and then opens and closes again. From just outside the elevator, he leans toward me, arm outstretched, offers an envelope.

I break my own rules and open it immediately (then wash my hands). A thank-you card. On one side, a photo of Dinah, a headshot, taken many years ago. Upswept hair, pearls, bright smile, like an ageing star of classic Hollywood. I stand the card on my mantel, light a candle in front of it.

Today's movie: *My Favourite Wife*

Day 25   520 deaths/16,563 cases

1 pound chicken (thighs).
1 onion, chopped (I use two).
1 clove garlic, chopped (I use two).
⅓ cup ketchup.
2½ tablespoons Worcestershire Sauce.
2½ tablespoons water.
2½ tablespoons A1 Sauce (Nico says I can substitute
   molasses or soy sauce. Soy sauce, it is).
1 tablespoon sugar (brown, for a bit of molasses).
1 tablespoon cider vinegar.

Cary Grant's slow-baked chicken, from a vintage celebrity cookbook. It's simple. Chicken, onions, garlic into the baking dish. Combine everything else into a sauce. Pour it over the chicken. Bake at low heat. Nico and I picked a day, coordinated cooking times.

OMG! I text. It smells so good.

I told you.

My stomach's grumbling. How much longer?

Patience.

We each set our own table with a lace tablecloth and our best china and crystal. The tablecloths were my Nonna's once. Mine is ivory, Nico's white. We rarely use them, but tonight has the hum of a holiday. We dress for dinner, laughing at the idea. Nico wears a clip-on bow tie and black suit, the closest he has to a tuxedo. I don my 1950s cocktail gown, black with red roses, bateau neckline, cinched waist, flared skirt. We're barefoot and laughing, imagining Cary Grant shaking his head in disapproval at our fashion faux pas. We position our laptops so we seem to sit across from each other. We mix champagne cocktails.

The chicken is moist, tender, falls off the bone. The savoury sauce has just a little heat. The caramelized onions melt in our mouths, sweet, soft, luscious.

We reminisce about the cruise we took before cruising became a death sentence, how we pretended we were Cary Grant and Deborah Kerr. We raise our glasses.

"If everything goes right," I begin, quoting our favourite scene. "In six months, you have a date."

"Where?" Nico grins.

"You pick the place."

"The top of the CN Tower. In six months. If it's safe."

"It'll be safe. And we'll be together. In person. Healthy."

"Hold the thought."

"Hold the thought."

Watch-party with Nico: *An Affair to Remember*

Day 28   **771 deaths/20,654 cases**

Before, during, or after the pandemic. Everything weighted and coloured forever.

Today's movie: *To Catch a Thief*

End of Month 1   1095 deaths/24,299 cases

Most patients want cameras on, some want them off, others prefer the phone. I use a virtual background, an orderly wall of books, to maintain the boundary between my home and my work. Headphones are too intimate, as if my patients' voices are inside me, so I use my computer's speakers. On the screen, they appear flat, unreal. Carl's wife refuses sex since lockdown started. Lou's husband won't help with childcare, homeschooling, or housework. They go on and on. My training has abandoned me. Listening is burdensome, exhausting in a way not true of in-person therapy. I nod empty sympathy, ask empty questions. We are probably all going to die, I want to say, but don't. I pretend my webcam has malfunctioned.

Today's movie: *Charade*

Mid-Month 2   4179 deaths/54,457 cases

Our first Christmas, she gave me an angel. Pink robe, beige wings, gold halo. Something you might order from Avon. Every December, I put it on the mantel, next to a smaller, rough-hewn wooden angel another patient carved years ago.

When I emailed I was reducing my hours during lockdown, she begged me not to abandon her.

Another Christmas, maybe three years ago, she gave me a picnic basket. Woven wicker, yellow gingham lining. Charming. Probably one of her thrift-store treasures. I used it for picnics on Ward's Island but found it cumbersome. Since then, it's been in my storage unit, in the building's sub-basement.

During our first phone psychotherapy session, she said she was afraid of her ICU patients, she didn't trust the PPE, she was sleeping in her basement to protect her children, she'd held a phone up to a dying man so his wife could say goodbye.

Last Christmas, she gave me a wooden tea-box. Blue paint distressed by actual age not some crafty effect. Once her mother's, then hers, now mine. She'd filled it with a variety of teas.

For our only video telemedicine session, I had the oolong tea and she had orange pekoe. That was all her nurse could find. She sat up in her hospital bed but was too weak, too feverish to continue for long. She was afraid of dying, of infecting her doctors, her nurses, and I offered no succour because I, too, was afraid.

Today, when the email from her husband arrives, I empty the tea-box and take it down to my storage unit. I dig her angel out of the Christmas decorations, put it into the tea-box. Then, I put the tea-box into the picnic basket. I lock her nesting gifts in that cluttered storage unit in that dank sub-basement.

Today's movie: *Penny Serenade*

Endless Month 2   5081 deaths/63,215 cases

1 package yeast dissolved in lukewarm water.
Salt, not too much.
Water, enough for a good dough.
3 handfuls flour. Nonna's handfuls, so 3¾ handfuls.

Mix wet into dry.

Good. Now knead.

Roll, fold, stretch the silky dough,
coaxing the gluten. Nonna, tell me
about the Spanish Flu. You must've
been scared, only sixteen years old.

Knead harder.

I remember your story about the
very sick, the hopeless, taken to the
field at the edge of the village. Waiting
on cots to die. Who did you lose?   *Not that hard or it
                                            wont rise.*

LUCIA GAGLIESE

I have so many questions, so many
things I wish I knew, I wish you'd
told me.

Did you forget the salt?

I did not forget the salt. Only forgot
it that one time. Thirty-two years
you've been gone. Tell me how I get
through this, that I will get through
this

*Without salt, it'll taste
like straw.*

There's enough salt. My hands ache.
Your hands were bigger, stronger
than mine. Long fingers, rounded
nails, arthritic knuckles, veins
raised like deep, dark rivers.

*Almost there. Keep
kneading.*

Your hands guided me across
busy streets, protected me in
crowds, comforted me from your
last hospital bed.

Good. Now shape it.

I smooth olive oil onto the
rounded dough. It's warm from
the work of my hands.

*Cover it. Leave it to rise.
Be patient.*

Every year, my hands look more
like yours.

Today's movie: *Topper*

70

Almost Month 3   **5822 deaths/70,091 cases**

Seeking human kindness. A sign. Hand-lettered. Held aloft by an older man, grey beard escaping from behind his mask. His clean clothes—khaki photographers' vest, cargo pants, Tilley hat—announce he is not homeless, not in need. He squats in front of the pharmacy. I watch from a safe distance. He holds up his sign, tries to make eye contact with the passersby. Most pretend not to see him. A few nod. None slow down. I approach. His eyes widen in welcome then fold into deep crows' feet. I exhale, nod. My shoulders drop.

Today's movie: *Only Angels Have Wings*

Month 3   **6452 deaths/75,959 cases**

I heave my trash bags into the dumpster in the garbage room, turn, and there's Adam, waiting six feet back, holding his recyclables. Adam and Andy live on my floor, just past the elevator. Adam, a retired cop well into his eighties, is still imposing, tall, broad-shouldered. "Well, well, how are you, young lady?" Menopausal lady is more accurate, but never mind.

We stand well-apart and gossip about our neighbours— who's wearing a mask, who isn't, who's going outdoors, who isn't. "I don't know how you do it, all alone," he says.

"Oh, I'm fine. Always been introverted, and with Facetime, Zoom, and whatnot, there's always company."

"And that's enough?"

"It has to be, right? I mean, the days are long. I see patients virtually. That's strange." Soon, I'm telling him that the days blur, that I haven't touched anyone in months, that I spend more time with Cary Grant than anyone else, and finally, through tears, that my favourite patient has died of COVID.

Adam listens, nods in sympathy, suggests walking in the valley, offers to join me, if we stay distanced and keep to his old-man pace.

71

I mumble garbled apologies and hurry from the garbage room.

That evening, there's a gentle knock on my door. I open it to find a shoebox. I disinfect it, lift the lid: one plastic-wrapped scone, three foil-wrapped chocolates, a half-full bottle of Canadian whisky, and a note, "Stockpile delicacies. You aren't alone, young lady."

Today's movie: *Room for One More*

It Seems Years   8470 deaths/100,043 cases

After three months of self-isolation, my thoughts zip along a freeway with countless on-ramps, off-ramps, lanes, choices. They enter and exit at dizzying speed. There are no fines for speeding, switching lanes without signalling, making U-turns, driving in circles. My thoughts do not decelerate on ramps, do not avoid blind spots, do not keep a safe distance between them. Buzzing and zipping all day, all night. Getting nowhere. Same roads, same curves, same on-ramps, same off-ramps. It is always and forever rush hour.

Today's movie: *Merrily We Go to Hell*

June 26, 2020   8730 deaths/104,629 cases

I'm baking myself a birthday cupcake. Chocolate. The package says *cake-in-a-mug*, but really, it's a cupcake. I empty the mix into my cheery, lemon-yellow mug. Add water and an egg. Stir. Microwave five minutes. It puffs up as it rotates, teeters on the brim, threatens to spill, deflates. A rotating cake lung. Inhale, exhale, inhale, exhale. When the microwave beeps, it deflates one last time. I frost it with Nutella.

All around the city, country, world, self-isolating birthday boys and girls, men and women celebrate. Perhaps their phones ring, their texts ping, their emails beep. But some, like me, celebrate in silence. I blow out the candle, wish for a vaccine.

Today's movie: *The Grass Is Greener*

Summer	**8806 deaths/106,643 cases**

Heat wave in isolation. Air conditioner broken. Too risky to call a repair person. In sports bra and boxer shorts, I move from room to room, chair to chair, seeking coolness. The balcony is too hot, except very early or very late in the day. I stay indoors, windows shut, curtains drawn, lights off. Without the sky, the view, I could be anywhere or nowhere. It could be anytime or no time. The days, months, seasons have all merged and blurred away.

I want to cry. About COVID, but not only COVID. There are many, many things to cry about. I don't know how to start. My shoulders hurt, clenched up around my ears. I try to drop them, pull them back. I will be a hunched old lady, rounded in on myself, as if I've caught a ball against my gut, as if I'm protecting my vulnerable soft spots. Like one of those bugs that curl up when they're afraid. What are they called? As children, we teased them by almost touching them. Those bugs, whatever they're called, curled up quickly, perfectly. Then we'd wait. Eventually, tentatively, the bug would uncurl. And we'd do it again.

Today's movie: *None but the Lonely Heart*

Still summer	**8978 deaths/115,789 cases**

I am safe, but my colleague-patients are on the front lines, battling this demon. Their lives shattered, they live in terror, yet persist. They seek my support. I can offer only telemedicine. As the weeks and months pass, my colleague-patients blend; their stories about their patients blend. Sometimes I can't tell them apart.

I am safe, but I am hiding. My colleague-patients' dedication leaves me feeling like a draft dodger, a coward in this

COVID war. Daily, they venture onto the battlefield while I stay home, sheltered.

I am safe, but I pretend to be a soldier. My colleague-patients imagine I'm like Jimmy Stewart, on hiatus from Hollywood, piloting B24 bombing missions over Nazi Germany, brave and tough for all his aw-shucks gentleness. But I'm nothing like Jimmy Stewart. I'm more like John Wayne, playing soldier. I parade around in my PPE uniform, tough, ready for anything, when really, I'm doing everything possible to avoid danger, avoid service. And just like Marion Morrison acting like the war hero John Wayne, I'm selling an image, a falsehood, a fantasy.

John Wayne was no Jimmy Stewart.

Today's movie: *The Philadelphia Story*

Dog Days   9074 deaths/122,053 cases

And I watch and remember when there was a whole other time, a whole other world.

Today's movie: *Once Upon a Time*

Third Sleepless Night   9124 deaths/125,408 cases

CovxietY
QuarantinEpidemiCoronaviruS
SymptomatiCougHypoxiAgeusiAnosmiAsymptomatiC
AerosolSpreaDropleToucHandSpikExposurElevatoR
RisKisSinGamblinGatherinGermSchooL
PrevenTestSoaProtectSwaBubbleSanitizE
TreatmentSurvivEffectiVEntilatoRespiratoR
ComorbiDiabetiClusteRNaughTransmissioN
VulnerablElderlYounGendeRacializeDisparitieS
FrontlinEssentiaLeadeR
PhysiciaNursEpidemiologisTraceResearcheR
LockdownStockpilinGrocerieSourdougHobbieS
StreaMovieSerieSeasoNetfliX

IsolateDespairinGrieFeaRemotEndurE
ZooMuteDistancEmployeDeliverieSavingSafEconomY
RecovereDeceaseD
PropagandAntivaxxeResistencE
PoliticS

Today   **9184 deaths/130,918 cases**

Nothing I try brings me any closer. The list of demands, tasks undone, grows exponentially. Emails, texts unopened, unread, unanswered. Fatigue. Lethargy. A sloth but without the equanimity. In this COVID-chaos, I've lost my drive, interest, motivation, pleasure. Everything I try fails. My sleep is broken. Up all night then fitful sleep through the day. My appetite is undisciplined. Chips, cakes, cookies, all day, every day.

I'm no help to my patients and cancel most of my appointments.

I don't read, go out, exercise. I yearn for my Nonna but ignore my friends, my family. Nico and I will not meet at the top of the CN Tower next month. Impossible. It's closed, the numbers too high, too dangerous. How foolish we were to think it would be over by now. I haven't watched a movie in two weeks. Ever since Cary Grant said, halfway through *People Will Talk*, that Mother Nature regularly tries to annihilate us all with catastrophes, pandemics, and plagues. I'd forgotten he said that. It was a shock, a betrayal.

I go from bed to bath to kitchen to recliner to bed to bath to kitchen to recliner. My life space has dwindled to nothing. This dwindling a dire warning, I know, but I can't reverse it.

Every night, I promise myself tomorrow will be different, but it never is.

This cannot be how it ends.

STRIPPED

Alice Gauntley

The game is Never Have I Ever. It is being played by a group of girls in a dorm room, the kind with beds set into painted-brick walls and graffiti scratched discreetly into corners. For the unfamiliar, the rules to the game are as follows: each person in turn states something they have not done. Everyone who has done the deed in question takes a drink. No one present knows who lives in this room—they have all come from other dorms, lured by the promise of a party. It doesn't matter; they hold their SOLO Cups loosely in their hands, and the game begins.

All the girls in this dorm room are strangers to each other. Here are the facts on playing Never Have I Ever with a group of strangers this size: four of the participants, on average, will be worried the others will think they have done too little, and the other three will be worried the others will think they have done too much. One person will lie, but most will relish the excuse to feel truths squeezed out of them. These are the numbers.

This time is no different. This time is statistically average. Nothing will happen this time that has not happened before.

The questions begin.

Never have I ever had anal sex. Seven bodies, seven tensions, ratcheting up or down as cups are raised to lips and giggles spill out of them in turn.

Never have I ever smoked weed. The group is starting to guess at each other's personalities. Assessments are being made.

Never have I ever failed a test. The power of confession coalesces in the spaces between their laughter. All the girls feel the pull of thread within them, the stitch of social fabric. They are all friends in this moment, although what will happen in the morning is anyone's guess.

Never have I ever left the country. A few girls think in awe of how many stories a body can hold. The others think only of the buzz in their limbs, their minds, and smile.

"Never have I ever done a striptease for someone," says one of the girls. It does not matter which one, because she is not one of the girls who has done it. She clarifies further: "I don't mean just taking off your clothes in front of everyone." (It is important to be precise in these matters). "I mean if you really put on a show."

Three girls raise their cups to their lips and drink. All drink deeply, one because she's gunning for the kind of night she won't remember tomorrow, one because she made her drink too weak, one because she doesn't know enough about alcohol yet to judge how she should pace these things.

A fourth girl raises her cup, then sets it back down. She makes a gesture with her hands, a kind of maybe-maybe-not, and an accompanying facial expression. "I'm not sure if I should drink for this one or not," she says.

"Ooh, I wanna hear this story!" says another girl. She will remember this as a bold move, a request reciprocated. Another girl cringes inwardly. She will remember this as a premonition.

The game is set aside for the moment. Seven bodies lean in closer in their circle on the dorm room floor. One girl is reminded of the time she and her elementary school friends formed a coven and tried to summon the spirit of one friend's dead grandmother. Another is reminded of Girl Scout camp fires.

The other girls do not think of anything, minds set to anticipation.

"My mom lives in an apartment building downtown," says the girl with the story, and she names the city she is from. "Our place is on the third floor, and my room has a window facing out across the street." Some of the girls can relate to this part of the story; some cannot.

"Across the street is a warehouse, or something. Anyway, no one lives there." The girl who thought of Girl Scout camp imagines the girl with the story raising a flashlight to her chin, illuminating her face at odd angles.

Some of the girls see where this is going now. Some do not. On all their tongues: the bitter sweetness of their fruit juice/ vodka blends.

The girl with the story continues, "So I change in front of the window. Right? I don't, like, draw the curtains or whatever. Sometimes, I guess, I just forget, but sometimes I like the idea that someone might see." One girl feels anxiety sink into her belly like a stone. Another girl feels a tug of desire between her legs. Yet another raises her cup to her lips, wanting to hide her facial expression, then lowers it, not sure if she is permitted to drink freely while the game is still in session.

"Sometimes I put on a show, a little," the girl with the story continues. "Nothing serious. Just dance a bit, bend over. Watch myself in the mirror. Remove my bra from one boob, pop it back, remove it from the other, like I saw one time when my mom took me to a burlesque show by mistake." No one else can relate to that part of the story.

The girl with the story speaks faster and faster. "And when I do that, I'm thinking, what if someone saw? What if some-one was watching from one of those warehouse windows after all, and I caused their sexual awakening, or I made them remember their youth, or something like that? What if I was a story they told someone, this girl and the way she moved her body, how much fun she looked like she was having?"

The story has momentum now. The story is in motion: up it goes. Soon the story will descend. Every girl in the circle knows this by now. Some are beginning to wish they were not here. Others are frozen in fear or fascination or both. Others are trying to compose a story of their own to rival this one, once this one girl's moment has passed.

"And then one day," says the girl, and she has enough of a sense of pacing to slow down, so all assembled lurch to a halt for one sickening moment before the story makes its vertical stomach-pit drop, "one day, I finished stripping, dancing around and everything. And then I was naked, and I looked out the window and down on the ground were two guys looking up at me. Watching me. And suddenly—" Here she pauses again, but this time she does not pause for dramatic effect, but rather because words leave her, language floating out the top of her head for a long moment before settling back into her body. And then her story plummets over the edge: "Two things happened at once. I knew I didn't like it. And I smiled as though I did."

Sick recognition tastes so similar to vodka and juice that several girls present cannot distinguish the sensations in their mouths. Others taste nothing familiar at all.

The girl who wanted to drink takes a long, slow sip. Every drinking game, after all, is about reaching a desired effect through turning the mechanism into a punishment. *Drink if you lose.* Each person in the circle has lost something, but some more so than others.

"What do you mean?" says one girl, who tastes no recognition mixed into her budget cocktail. "Why did you smile?"

"I don't know," says the girl with the story. "But I just kept smiling, and I kept getting ready for bed. I bent over to pick up my pajama top from the floor, I mean, it was just a T-shirt, really. And I felt bad about that, that it wasn't a sexy thing, that

I wouldn't be fun to watch once I put it on. I stared the two guys in the eye and slipped it over my head."

She has not told this story before, although she has, in other circumstances, shared stories that have made other people decide not to become her friend. She did not tell the story the way she meant to, but she cannot pinpoint where it veered off the rails.

"So what happened next?" says a girl who has not spoken yet. She is trying to get the story back on track, because it seems like the best way to move past it. She holds a cup of water as well as alcohol, and she counts her drinks.

"Then I closed the curtains and went to bed. And only then—that was when I realized I didn't want to smile at the guys. Or, like, that was when I listened to myself about it."

Outside the room, there is music, there is chanting, there is laughter on top of laughter on top of drunken jokes. A few girls wish they had not closed the door so the party would not feel so far away. The night is lurching away from them all, tilting like the walls the moment before you pass out.

The girl with the story fills the silence, of course. Several girls wonder if this is something she always does: fill awkward pauses with awkward words. Several others want to cry but aren't sure why, just that this story is tugging at something inside them, making them aware of their skin like the first time someone whistled at them on the street.

"So," says the girl with the story, raising her glass, "does that count as a striptease or not?"

DEAD BIRDS

Don Gillmor

Four years after Liz and Bennett were married, she got a job at the Reference Library, working in the religious silence of the rare books room, enclosed by glass. The people who came there weren't allowed to make notes with pens; that indelible proximity was a threat to the collection. Liz issued them short pencils and white muslin gloves so the essential oils that lingered on their fingers didn't deteriorate the delicate pages. People automatically whispered when they came in; the atmosphere demanded reverence.

She saw a certain type: the kind of people who were more interested in ideas than appearances, for example. And people for whom the past held a deep, authentic living interest. They could sit with those texts for hours. There were people doing research and those who she suspected weren't doing research, who came only for that mood of sanctity, the sense of ancient dust settling on them. It was a curious, largely unvaried crowd. So when Thomas Meechum came in, he seemed out of place. It's true that he wore a tweed jacket and sensible shoes, but he had a robust quality that wasn't often seen in that room. He had thick, prematurely greying hair and his face was strong and angled and almost tanned rather than off-white and vaguely collapsed, like many of those around him. He had a muted athleticism—not like someone who went to a gym, more like someone you'd see hiking through the Scottish Highlands. He came in looking for the Audubon Collection, the series of 435 hand-painted engraved prints of North American birds. A copy had been bought by the library in 1903, purchased for $1,900, a fortune back then. The prints had degraded over the years, and the folio had been withdrawn from public use, though Meechum had managed to get limited access.

He came regularly and their dealings became codified, a hushed greeting, the issuing of gloves and pencil. He filled out the form requesting what he needed, then she retrieved it. At some point while he was working, he would look up and catch her attention and she would come to his table and he would whisper something, a question, a request. She began to look forward to seeing him, to touching him briefly on the forearm, whispering, her lips inches from his ear.

She became familiar with his scent (you weren't allowed to wear cologne or perfume in the rare books room). She knew his voice, but only the whispered version; she'd never heard his regular speaking voice. In that silence, in that lulling sepia light, it felt vaguely clandestine.

It was two months before they spoke to one another in normal voices. She left for her lunch break and he followed and asked (still whispering) if she wanted to join him for lunch. They went around the corner to a small café that offered healthy sandwiches and organic soups. Liz's lunch was in her purse, the lunch she had hastily and imperfectly made while trying to get Tyler ready for daycare and trying to get him to eat something—*anything*—and settling finally, with a sense of failure that almost produced tears, on a bowl of animal crackers and chocolate milk.

"I just wanted to thank you for all your help up there," he said in a normal voice, a rich baritone that suited him. He held out his hand. "Thomas." Though of course she already knew his name.

"Liz. And it's nothing," she said. "My job."

"You're very good at it."

"What is it, exactly, that you're doing?" she asked.

"I'm re-examining Audubon as a metaphor for America. He was self-made, vain, a natural salesman. He becomes famous, moves to New York, loses his mind and is dead at sixty-five. It resonates with what's happening now. I mean: there's my book on a platter."

Liz wasn't sure that it was. It seemed a little pat, and there were already two Audubon biographies that she knew of, but she was drawn to Meechum's enthusiasm. When he spoke, his hands moved symphonically: small repeating circles interspersed by sharp expansive gestures, like the percussion coming in. Liz had spent quite a bit of time with the Audubon book. It was one of their most prized possessions. She knew Audubon had shot the birds himself, then stuffed them and wired them into those poses. So many of them were extinct now: passenger pigeon, great auk. There were more.

"Audubon was rich," Thomas went on. "Then he was poor. And what was the antidote to bankruptcy? Greatness! That's when he decides to do this book, this insane, ambitious project. He's out wandering the land with a shotgun and a box of paints. He used to give dancing lessons."

Liz had always thought of him as essentially French rather than American. She wasn't surprised by the dancing lessons. What she had noticed about Audubon's birds was how animated they were. It wasn't how birds were painted back then. Especially so-called scientific paintings, which tended to be sterile and one-dimensional. Audubon's birds were part of a narrative, they were alive. There was something weirdly human about some of them. Audubon loved birds, had loved them his whole life. Then he spent all his time killing the thing he loved. Liz supposed that was an American trait.

"And what do you see in those paintings?" She sounded like an interviewer.

"What I see ... I see the country growing up in his image. Wild, foreign, at home in the woods, filled with dreams of riches. Then it goes to New York and goes crazy and dies. Audubon couldn't have been more American if he'd invented baseball."

Thomas went on for another fifteen minutes and then looked at his untouched soup. "But I'm boring you," he said.

"No, not at all." Her goat cheese and sprout sandwich on thick whole grain bread was mercifully gone. "I've always loved Audubon's birds."

"They're easy to love."

She went home that day with a sense of lightness that she was careful not to define. As she sat at the small round dinner table, watching Bennett chew through an overcooked pork chop, as she looked down at Tyler, who had distributed his cut-up version around his tray like a Druid ritual, she thought there might be something more than this. Not necessarily instead of this. But another layer. One of the surprises of motherhood was the absence of a private life, which seemed to have been squeezed out of her. She was a receptacle for her child's needs and her husband's vagueness. The next morning she showered carefully, and discarded two outfits before choosing one that was flattering but wouldn't look as if she had spent time trying to choose an outfit. In the subway, she examined the faces around her and wondered about the regrets that trailed after them like smoke.

When she and Thomas finally slept together, almost six weeks later, it seemed like the natural culmination of what had been a very delicate and incremental seduction. He was more attentive in bed than Bennett, though perhaps a bit bold for what was, strictly speaking, a first date. And she found this slightly intoxicating. It was, she supposed, precisely what an affair was supposed to be, though she was cautious not to use the word. After they made love, he got out of bed and walked to the desk by the window and picked up some pages. He was older than Liz, but very fit. His penis was darker than Bennett's. Perhaps that was what made it seem larger. He got back under the covers and began to read. "John James Audubon, né Jean Jacques Audubon, was above all, a salesman. He was a tireless self-promoter. He *was* America: talented, wild, awkward and brazen at the same time, a naturalist, a killer. He embodied every contradiction of this new land."

Thomas read for half an hour, and in that half hour, Liz realized that his book might not be very good. His thesis, she had come to appreciate, was a good one. But his execution was a bit clumsy. He wanted to get to his point too quickly, he would use every aspect of the man's life to prove the authorial point. She stared at his hands—the hands of someone who had done manual labour but had used moisturizer—and she listened to his voice and felt like she was back in university, and their lives were ahead of them and they were filled with revolutionary ideas and stupid hope.

When he finished, he turned to her and it was clear to Liz that he had no doubts about his work, that he felt it was brilliant, that he expected praise rather than an opinion.

"I liked the part about him posing the passenger pigeons as lovebirds," she said carefully. "I mean they used to darken the sky there were so many. And now they're extinct. And maybe somehow he saw it coming, and there's some kind of lovely awful irony in there."

Thomas's face clouded slightly. "I doubt he was being ironic."

"It's good," Liz added.

"Yes."

After four months, the affair had assumed a regularity. They met every Tuesday and every second Thursday. They went to his apartment, which was a pleasant fifteen-minute walk from the library. His initial interest in her life, his questions, disappeared. He was like a census-taker; he took down vital information, but hadn't really prepared any follow-up questions (Are you happy? Where is this going? How old is your son?).

At home, Liz made a series of rationalizations:

1. She was in a better mood since the affair began, which benefitted both Bennett and Tyler.
2. She was a more adventurous lover, also a benefit to Bennett—or would be if they had a sex life.
3. Because she had assumed most (all) of the duties of child-rearing, she deserved this.
4. While Bennett probably wasn't having an affair, he almost certainly would at some point.
5. She would regret it if she didn't.
6. She could end it at any time.

When she and Bennett first started dating, he told her he was going to write a book on the Cold War. He'd written the first line, which he recited to her and which she still remembered: "It was 1962 and the bombs strained against their leashes like rabid Dobermans." After Bennett had landed the job of history professor at the university, they drank wine and mapped out their lives in vivid detail. In retrospect they had spent more time mapping their lives than actually living them, though perhaps it was a trick of perspective. Now Bennett hated his job. He hated the university bureaucracy, his distracted students and his malignant Dean. And he hated his unwritten book and resented her for being a witness to that void.

On a Thursday in November, the weather grey, her mood sour after dropping a squalling Tyler off at daycare, then made worse by a suffocating day in the rare books room (her days always too loud and too quiet), she arrived at Thomas's apartment not remotely in the mood for sex. When he began to take off his clothes she told him she really wasn't feeling up to it. His shirt was unbuttoned and he turned to her and she could see he almost uttered the words Well why did you come here then? It took him a few minutes to adjust. He buttoned his shirt with an actual sigh of resignation and plodded over to the desk and picked up a sheaf of papers and then stood in his small living room and began to read. He paced as he read, which she found pompous and annoying. "Audubon lived what Alexis de Tocqueville observed—the birth of a nation that was relentless in its appetites, sprawling in its canvas, a contradictory stew that would, inevitably, turn against itself." When he finished, he dropped the pages to his side and looked at her.

Liz waited a full ten seconds before saying anything. She felt punished by his readings. "I think you have to be subtler in your approach, Thomas," she said. "Your point is a good one. But I think you're hammering the reader over the head with it. You could let it develop a bit. Show his life, let the reader draw a few of these conclusions on her own, then underline them."

It was her first overt criticism of his work. He stared at her for almost a minute. "You mean just deliver up a straight biography. It's been done, Liz. Read Hart-Davis, read Souder."

"I'm not suggesting a straight biography. But I'm worried the reader will feel she's being force-fed. A bit. Look, it's a wonderful book, Thomas. I just think you should have a little more confidence in the reader."

"Readers are idiots." He was pacing again.

"That hasn't been my experience. And I've met a few," she said dryly.

"This is a book of *ideas*," he said forcefully.

Liz wondered if the singular wouldn't be more appropriate. One idea. She examined him, a thirty-eight-year-old man writing a mediocre book that might not be published.

He lived in a serviceable apartment and pretended to know more about wine than he actually did. She realized she had embarked on the affair without any real motive. It was the seduction that she had most enjoyed. In retrospect, those weeks where they circled one another in the library, whispering, complicit in something that didn't yet exist, that had been the best part. His voice in her ear, her hand on his arm. The anticipation.

Her marriage wasn't a disaster. She was neither unhappy or happy with Bennett. Their lives were rote, and the explosion of having a child had settled into a new roteness. It had fallen to her, all those feedings, the changing of clothes, the lulling to sleep, the buying of formula and toys and diapers and finding daycare. Bennett managed to seem helpful, but in fact he wasn't. Motherhood had isolated her somehow, a surprise. That you bring another life into the world and it made you feel more alone. It didn't help that Tyler wasn't an easy child. He wasn't naturally affectionate; he squirmed out of arms that tried to hold him. He carried an almost existential indifference within him, if that was possible for a boy of two, if that wasn't a heretical motherhood thought (of which she'd had quite a few).

And then she went to work in the rare book room, a room enclosed by glass. The irony wasn't lost on her. She was pinned under glass, a specimen, desiccating, trapped. Instead of an affair, she'd managed to find a second marriage. Or this was the trajectory of every relationship. This was love.

The light outside Thomas's window was grey. November had a bleakness matched only by February, though at least February had the decency to be short. The light inside was grey too. On his wall, Thomas had a print of Audubon's American robin, a family of them, the mother and father pitching in, the baby with its mouth open, waiting to be fed. She remembered the dead robin she'd found in their backyard as a child. It had probably hit the window and broken its neck. It lay there, soft, intact. She picked it up and took it into their garage and made a nest using a cardboard box and a dishcloth. She squeezed milk into its beak from an eyedropper and read it a story. She believed that she could bring it back to life through her compassion and untapped magical powers, that it would become her friend, would follow her everywhere and appear out of the sky and land on her hand in the schoolyard and amaze the world.

She wished she could tell Thomas this story, that they would be lying in bed after making love and she could tell him about the robin. But she knew she couldn't. Her story would be met with indifference. There wasn't room for another dead bird.

She felt suddenly weary, the bone weariness she'd had when she was breastfeeding Tyler and was half-asleep all the time. Thomas was still standing in the middle of the living room, reluctant to give up the stage. His face held the petulant hurt that Tyler's had when she took something dangerous away from him.

She walked to the subway in the awful November light. Dozens of people in dark winter coats moved through the gloom with their heads down. A snowflake fluttered in front of her, the first of the season. She looked up, expectant. In the streetlight, thousands of snowflakes hovered above her like moths, suspended, as if they were afraid to fall.

LADY WITH THE BIG HEAD CHRONICLE

Angélique Lalonde

1. Lady with the Big Head in the Garden

The lady with the big head is out there in the misty morning. Is she wearing a veil? What is she doing in my garden? The mist is sitting on the river, slightly spread over the land. I see the mountain beyond, and the lady with the big head stooped over my onions. Not like yesterday when the mist was so thick I wouldn't have seen her if she were there.

Was she out there yesterday, picking calendula seeds to save for next season? She didn't ask me if she could tend my garden while I am in the house doing other things. She's never talked to me at all. She avoids me if I try to approach her, floating off into the mist or the memory of mist, then reappearing later doing different things in different places. I saw her digging at an anthill with the bear that has been hanging around our yard. She used a stick and the bear used her big broad paws.

The lady with the big head was helping the bear, or the bear was helping the lady with the big head, I'm not sure which. Either way they were digging up the anthill near the apple tree. I didn't mind that. I had noticed the ants were in

93

the sickly tree crawling all around and that probably was not a good sign, so maybe the lady with the big head and the bear were helping the apple tree too?

She might be taking some onions, or weeding, or eating slugs. I can't tell exactly what she is doing because of the veil that hangs down from her big head over her body and drapes on the ground, hiding her movements. Also the light has not yet come, only a faint blueness and all that mist. I could offer her a hot tea but if I walk out there she'll float away from me.

Later I'll go look and see if she's taken onions or left any knick-knacks. Once I found a golden spool of thread so strong, fine and shiny, I knew it was magical. The kind of thread that could be used to build spider webs that are always visible no matter the light. Visible but still translucent, an ephemeral quality of there and not quite there, only gold instead of silver. It might be what she makes her veil out of, or at least what she uses to mend the veil, because now that I think of it the veil is not golden, it's more of a purple-grey shadow. Sometimes she has it pulled back and I can almost make out her features as she goes about doing things ladies with big heads do. She looks a little bit like me and a little bit like Rod Stewart, which is an odd mix for a lady. A couple of times I've glimpsed her looking like my dog, John Black, who died last winter. She might have taken her skull from the forest where we left the dog's body to use as a mask; it seems like something the lady with the big head would do.

2. Lady with the Big Head and the Weight of her Head

The lady with the big head is having trouble holding her head up. It's dipping forward this week, jutting at the chin. A chiropractor would look at her and shudder, thinking of her unhappy spine, contorted and compressed by the heaviness of gravity. He would want to brace her somehow, crack her in all sorts of places, and have her do little exercises with devices of his own making to relieve the pressure on her neck.

Who can she consult for this, living as she does in the forest? Being only partway real? Who would book her in for an appointment with her lack of proper name and no address to speak of? No email or phone number to confirm a correct time? Who would make a call to the forest, following her trail to find where she is sleeping and wrench that crook from her neck? How would she pay them? Would a chiropractor accept dried mushrooms in payment for his services? Would he treat without an X-ray showing the insides of the lady with the big head's troubled bones? Instead we build her a device from which she can hang upside down, with a long flat back that inverts once she's strapped herself in. I hang there a lot when she's not using it, feeling the blood pool in my head, imagining my spine unkinking so more of my life can bubble up through that crazy central nerve cluster that sends messages all through my body, making it so I can know.

3. Lady with the Big Head has a Dream

She had a quiet dream, the lady with the big head. It was quiet so she kept sleeping. If it had been a loud raucous dream she would have startled herself out of it. She does not want to dream raucous dreams. Still, she does. Sometimes she seeps in my window and makes me dream them too.

She dreams she is living in a musty apartment where the shower runs straight onto the carpet and there are old patio umbrellas stacked in the storeroom. Enough of them that there is no room to store her own things. There are also a few toilets side by side, some of them with equipment attached to them for various kinds of disabilities. The lady with the big head does not want to live in this apartment. She wipes up dust and pubic hair gathered around the toilets that was not cleaned away before she moved in. She wonders why she is paying rent here when it has not been cleaned of other people's pubic hair, and the landlord is storing things in her storeroom. There are two bathtubs side by side in another part of the apartment, one slightly lower than the other. The lower one has a rack in it like a water bath canner and is very dirty. The lady with the big head pours two baths and gets in the cleaner one. She is happy to have a bath in the dream. She is in the bath with a friend who is living down the hall and tells her not to get in the lower bath because it is filled with other people's filth.

Later the lady with the big head wakes up and goes around the forest. She doesn't live in a musty apartment. She doesn't have a bath and there is soil everywhere. It does not seem soiled. She goes down to the cold river and washes her face. Some of it washes right off. The lady with the big head is going around with only part of a face today, refreshed to be kept so clean by the world. A new face will grow back, it always does, who knows what it will look like? Part of her face will look like her old face and part of her face will be her new face. She follows the cycle of the moon. As the moon wanes the rest of her old face will peel off in fragments. In the darkest night of the new moon she'll be wiped clean of that old face and her new face will be there, coming to fruition over the next few weeks toward some kind of whole. During full moon she glows with the fullness of her features, distinct for such a short window of time. If you didn't already know her by the size of her head, you'd know her then by the flicker and fullness of her face.

4. Lady with the Big Head Knits

The lady with the big head has started a new knitting project. She has gathered mycelia from the underside of leaves, dried it, weaving in lichens hanging from pine trees, grasses dried before they harden too much to be malleable, licks of the thinnest birch and hazel branches. All strung together and rolled into balls. The lady with the big head is knitting a fine gown and a warm blanket. She is knitting a scarf and toque for the mangy squirrel that lost much of its coat to mites this summer. She gathers bits of feather and tufts of fur scattered in the forest from fresh coyote kills, along the roadside from smashed up deer and grouse. These she loops in for warmth and softness amongst the brittle structures of plant and fungus parts.

5. Lady with the Big Head Pilfers Garlic

The lady with the big head is digging a hole for the winter. Last year's burrow collapsed because of all of the rain. She has borrowed our shovel, which we had hoped to use to prepare the ground for garlic. The lady with the big head mostly leaves the garlic alone. We put out a few bundles in the barn so that she will not dig up our seed. One year we lost almost our whole harvest to her, but we learned that if we made an offering she would leave the stuff in the ground alone.

She wants us to have our garlic but if there is not enough to go around she will pilfer. She needs the garlic to keep her belly warm over the long winter. To spice up the plain roots she keeps stored in her caches and the cambium she munches in leaner times.

The lady with the big head knows how to make fires. Probably she knows how to start them from flints, but she also takes matches and lighters. Either it's her or our son William, who is trying to hide his pyrotechnic activities. William assures us he's seen her smoking whatever brand of cigarettes she can get her hands on and tossing the butts under the pine tree where she thinks no one will see them. When we buy a 3-pack of strike-anywheres from the hardware we always leave a pack sealed in Ziploc out in the barn in the cubby set aside for offerings, to make things a little easier for her.

Sometimes she leaves things for us in return—bits of woven grass or the skeletons of small animals, any garbage William leaves out in the bush with his friends when they're out there being dickheads. Probably they think it's funny that the lady with the big head will pick up after them. But we warn them to be careful, as she's not a custodian. She has a streak of righteousness to her, and one way or another, we tell William, something bad will come of his carelessness if he keeps goading her.

6. Lady with the Big Head Reads Poetry

Does the lady with the big head suffer from heartburn? It is hard to say because her body is such a mystery. Perhaps that big head weighs down on her organs, making acid rise up her esophagus to burn her throat? Or perhaps because of her healthful diet of herbs, roots, plants, and small animals, she is safe from such refluxes? One thing we know is that the lady with the big head is a big admirer of poetry. We leave volumes for her in the barn because she knows better than to accept gifts from us directly. In the beginning when we left books out she would take them and not bring them back. We lost several of our favourite poets that way and are still uncertain where they've gone. There would be no way for her to keep the books from rotting out there with all the dampness. Without insulated walls and ongoing fires or electric baseboards, things out there won't keep. They'll rot and rust and be taken over by mosses, their original words and functions becoming unreadable. So even if she has kept them, they are still lost to us, and will become lost to her also. Unless of course she is able to commit them to memory, which is highly possible with that big head of hers that must have so much room in it for stories about the world.

We have long discussions in our home about what volume to offer up next, how to pick poets for the lady with the big head's attunement to the literary world. William writes out pages of his favourite hip hop rhymes so that she'll be in the know about different kinds of verse, not just filled up with the tender shit his mothers are into. She leaves us the spectres and voices of the nonhuman to learn as we leave her the leavings of those who play and build with the language the colonizers left us. Who knows how many misunderstandings pass between us? And truthfully we have no education in poetry. Only the internet and the suggestions put forth by the surveillance of our previous choices to offer us other things we might like based on the things we have chosen before. Also a pitiful section of poetry in our local library, which nonetheless we are grateful for. Sometimes our friends will send us things from the cities in which they live where human words sprawl over the landscape. Here many of those words are washed away or covered in brush as soon as they arrive, unable to convey the poets' observations about human-scaled landscapes and being. The land here eats everything. There are, after all, so many intact spirits roaming, and they are hungry for knowing. The lady with the big head is a little bit like a medium between us and this world. We fumble toward knowing one another with our gifts and intentions, undaunted by our failures to understand one another. Thrilled by the revelations that come.

7. Lady with the Big Head Shares her Kill

It is unclear whether or not the lady with the big head has children. Many creatures follow her around and participate in her doings. Two ravens perch in a poplar to watch her handiwork as she cuts across the grouse's neck and holds its feet to rip the skin off. She keeps the breasts and feathers and tosses the rest of it to the ravens. She's not greedy, makes sure to share what she is gifted from the world.

After ripping as much flesh as they can get, the ravens get wind of another kill, take off in the direction of death. The lady with the big head continues wandering, tomorrow she plans to spend all day at the river reading rocks, testing the words of lichen with her practiced tongue.

8. Lady with the Big Head's Sexuality

The lady with the big head was not human before she became a partway ghost, which is why I chide Alma, calling her "my prudish wife," when she is disgusted by the lady with the big head's sexuality. This morning after licking dew from cabbage fronds, the lady with the big head fornicated with a giant raven in the yard, making us think maybe she consorts with gods. Her screams had us rushing outside, thinking the cat had been attacked by coyotes. Our son William got out his smart phone, trying to make a video, but luckily we were on him before he could make it to the cell booster for a signal. We confiscated the phone and erased any traces of an encounter that was never meant to be made into media, then had a good talk about respecting people's boundaries. He argued that the lady with the big head and the raven are not really people and if they are they should be a little more discreet about where they decide to fuck.

We reminded William that despite legal title, we're encroaching on territory that has boundaries chronicled in stories that have never been told to us, and maybe the lady with the big head is part of that world. Or maybe she isn't. There is so much we cannot know because of the knowledge we have been born into, passed down through the direct or banal violence of our immigrant ancestors. It may be that she has been here so very long, as ancient as the land, or perhaps she came with us or with some other settlers from another part of the world and got marooned here and goes on living, even though the humans that once knew her are gone or dead and their children do not remember? We do not know how to ask, or who to ask, and the lady with the big head is not telling. But William is fourteen and immersed in dominant cultural values (despite our best efforts) so he doesn't get these discrepancies. He's all over what's mine and not mine, thinking you can really own things, that legal possession gives you alienable rights that exclude other truths from the land.

Alma isn't sure how the lady with the big head's sexual life will affect William's burgeoning sexuality. This morning it was the raven and last week we saw her sensually stroking a vixen's back, the purr from her throat unmistakable. Alma's been keeping William inside lately because of the birch bark etchings that have been popping up on the trails. The kind of images that make me shiver down there, making me so uncomfortably aroused that shame clamps me down before the pleasure can spread any further. The lady with the big head depicts the erotic life of forest creatures in ways that enliven our human erogenous zones. We find ourselves arguing in bed about whether she is being vulgar or artful out there in the forest all around.

9. Lady with the Big Head's Perspective on Identity

The lady with the big head does not really care about technologies of identity construction and the limited dialects of culture inherent in dominant practices of person-making. Meaning comes to her through languages of texture and heeding. Quicksight-and-categorize is not the primary way she has learned to become among others like or unlike her. Therefore she categorizes differently.

There are so many ways of likeness.

The lady with the big head interrelates intimately with many beings and because of this the plain sufferings of humans fall in line with the plain sufferings of salmon, hummingbird, lichen, salamander, and snail.

Watching her out there limping I can see that the lady with the big head has become very angry that the plain sufferings of salmon have become so much less plain through the grasping patriarchy of capital and conquest, as we go on taking and taking and taking from this world in the drive to constantly remake ourselves.

The lady with the big head is listening for silenced voices. Sometimes I wish she would start yelling in a big ghost voice that causes terrible reverberations in order to frighten away surveyors who fly around in helicopters trying to decide how to pipe bitumen and gas under the land to put it in big leaky ships across oceans so that more cheap plastic goods can be manufactured to accumulate dangerously in the world. That her voice alone could change this.

But maybe that's just me, inventing motivations and capabilities for her? Maybe in my looking I am like others like me—an accident or designed outcome of the generations that came before? Left here with garbled stories because each generation tries to efface or correct the stories of the last in our attempts to settle ourselves. The stories that bind us to place, transformed with each displacement. Solid as we claim ourselves to be, we are deeply unsure what to do with the buried stories that froth forth into our fields of perception. Stories that link us uncomfortably to the violent displacements that have made this home. We writhe with our inability to make meaning as the lady with the big head voyages along the dendritic trails of her manifold histories.

10. Lady with the Big Head Intuits Ice

The lady with the big head intuits ice as a long pause in the body of the world. She knows it's not really like that because ice is dynamic, changing itself constantly as the world around it fluctuates, loosening its bonds and flowing away or tightening toward itself and heaving into space. Marching to cover land-masses and bust open rock. Not really a self at all, able to exist as water or vapour. Becoming forceful and epic, becoming vastness, becoming the body of the world, breaking the body of the world into infinitesimal fragments which it devours or gestates. Always in flux with the stuff that makes land.

The lady with the big head tries to parse out the spirit bits. The enlivened elements. She sticks her hand into ice and has to pull back because it's just so cold! She sticks her hand into water and animalcules cling to her, blotching her skin, nibbling her cells. The water is so inviting she plops herself in, grateful for a big head that floats like a buoy. Her limbs fall below, but her breathing hole must be kept out or water will clog her and push out her spirit, turning her body to fodder. She cannot live in water, cannot live without water. So unlike salamander who doesn't need to keep constant temperature, like salamander too, rhythmically heaved by breath. She reaps the benefits of pulse. But because she is only somewhat alive she can pause herself like ice for eons, fragmented, covering up the cities we made that we thought would last forever, turning them into questions for future creatures that come after the ice.

11. Lady with the Big Head Tells Me to Shut the Fuck Up

I think I hear the lady with the big head whispering. Maybe she is telling me to shut the fuck up? Not for just one hot second, or three timed minutes registered in my meditation app and logged online to be compared with others like me that have become so aware of their mindfulness? Maybe she just keeps saying shhh, shhhh, shhhh, like we used to whisper to William when he was a baby and crying all the time, needing to be soothed by his mothers' warm soft breaths? Maybe she is saying that it is so hard to hear when we are always stating

things, crashing about the multi-voiced world with our so loud
authoritative claims and combustion engine machinery?

> then it goes that you get real quiet for a real long
> time, no one knows how long, and there are a lot of
> things you hear, and then maybe after a long time
> there is a sound that moves you. not like

moving in your limbs to get things done, but
another kind of moving, one that comes from inside
the body. real deep in there, maybe a little bit close
inside between the lungs and heart where there is
all that breathing and blood pumping, and there
you get moved, still real quiet, because you're trying
not to make it about your words and your knowing,
make place for another kind of being, like moving
with instead of moving *about*.

> you're out there in her garden and she's making a hole
> with her fingers in the soil. you've got to respect her veil
> but it's hard not to want so much to peek inside. you tease
> apart the root bulb, hand her one piece, then another. she is
> asking you only to break up the

bulb and hand her the parts one by one. she is not moving away
from you as long as you break up the bulb
> and hand her the parts one by one.
>> (without pressing your narratives in,
>>> assuming you might know
>>>> how to know her world).

ARNHEM

Elise Levine

I keep thinking: two girls on a hill. I forget where. Heidelberg, or Conwy in North Wales where there's also a castle. Two girls making fast along a wet street. Oxford or Bruges. Us, they're thinking, telepathic as ants. One girl's freezing in her white summer dress. The other girl's wearing army surplus pants and a baggy turtleneck sweater. They're seventeen, smug as cats. They've blown off the archeological dig on Guernsey for which they'd secured positions six months earlier by mail. Mud labour, fuck that shit! On the appointed start date they simply hadn't shown. Instead they're hitchhiking around, doing all the things.

They order frites in a fancy café in Brussels, which arrive on a silver platter, grease soaking into the paper doily. North of Lisbon they sleep on a beach one night. They run out of money in Paris and panhandle, not very well, but they get by.

Who do they think they are?

Who did I?

I think we went to the zoo in Arnhem. I think we met a composer at some youth hostel who was from Arnhem. We met two young Italian men at a hostel in Mons. No one else was around and they tried to kiss us that night near the bathrooms when we went to brush our teeth. One of them forced one of us against the wall of the repurposed army barracks and thrust his pelvis a few strokes while the other one stood back with the other one of us and watched. In Amsterdam there was a phone call for one of us and we trundled barefoot down the hostel stairs to the office in our prim cotton nighties. Turns out one of our grandmothers was dying, the grandmother of the one of us who still had a grandmother.

I was the friend. We were friends. I forget why I'm telling this. I go to the corner store for ice cream. I sit on my couch, off the clock since I lost my job. My husband. Already I forget why. It's so easy. My apartment sparkles, I kid not. I try to count on my one hand how many ideas I still have from back then. On my other hand, add the few new.

I think how long ago it seems that I slept beside her in a roomful of older young women, all of us on cots half a foot off the damp floor. This was Cambridge. Dew on the windows all night, late June. The women were real diggers, by day excavating a nearby pre-Roman site. Down the hall, the men diggers, including my friend's older brother who we were visiting, slept in another large room. I don't remember much about the men but the women were solid, practical, tough. Intimidating to the extent that when I say I slept, the truth is I barely did, cold, legs aching, bladder wretched but I was too scared to get up. To be weak. Or weaker to even think it.

Which one was I?

Not the one in the summer dress. The one in the Shetland turtleneck.

*

The next morning in Mons the sky was clear. Awake for much of the night, we rose early and packed and picked through the continental breakfast array in the main hall. Individual portions of spreadable cheese wrapped in foil. I'd never seen anything like it. Nor the crisp rye flatbreads. The Belgian couple who managed the hostel, in their mid-thirties probably, kindly asked how we'd slept. We spilled the beans and the couple's eyes grew round and their foreheads pinched. They would speak to those two young Italian men.

By the time they did, if they did, and it's true we believed them, we were gone.

*

We left Lisbon broke and caught rides up the coast. Mostly guys, some with their own ideas. Sometimes a woman who'd ask if we were okay. We were okay.

*

The beach was small with large-grained sand. Brown, I recall. I can't remember if we even bothered to take our shoes off.

The man who drove us there was slight of build. His mustache was light brown. At dusk he parked on the street and led us down to the water where we thanked him and said goodbye. He'd asked if we wanted to sleep on a beach that night and we'd said yes please. Anything for an adventure to recall later in life, as in how cool was that?

The sea frothed at our feet and the air smelled of brine. We toed a few half circles and the sea erased them. We stretched our backs, yawned. He refused to take the hint. Thank you, okay? He made himself understood then. He was spending the night with us. He'd called a friend at the roadside café he'd taken us to earlier, where we'd eaten squid in black ink very cheap and drunk cheap wine. Soon his friend would be here to meet us too.

It's not like the driver had a tent or sleeping bags.

Was there a moon that night? There was a family camping nearby. A woman, a man, a child maybe eight-nine years old. They had a tent. Sleeping bags, no doubt. Judging by the track marks, they'd dragged a picnic table over, and the fire on their portable stovetop burned brighter while the sky grew darker and the man and my friend and I sat on the sand waiting, he for his friend, my friend and I for some notion of what to do, clueless as sheep.

A flashlight made its way toward us. It was the woman. With her nearly no English and our no Portuguese and a little French between us, she ushered my friend and I into the tent with her husband and son.

How did we all fit? I must have slept the sleep of the dead, for all I can remember of the rest of that night.

*

When we first got together, my husband, who moved out last Saturday, complained that I slept like a bird. When things went from infrequently to occasionally bad to totally the worst, he said I slept like a fruit fly.

I pull the covers over my head. Good thing I brought my cell phone with me, light in darkness, all that. I hit his number. Hang up when he answers. He immediately calls back, probably to yell.

Stop calling me, I text-beg. Please.

For at least the next hour, while I still have my phone on, and for the first time in several years, he does as I say.

Later I'm running a bath and thinking again about the beach in Portugal, the family's tent.

The next morning we woke and the driver lay curled like an inchworm on the sand near the waterline, no friend in sight.

He drove us back to the highway, game of him. We girls, young women, once again stuck out our thumbs. Auto-stop, they call it there.

My husband has never once in his life hitchhiked. He's in IT. Like never even tried? No, he said on our first date, dinner at a pasta bar before a movie. Pale noodles, pale sauce, what can you expect for Cleveland, I thought, having recently moved there for the second of what turned into a seemingly endless stream of visiting assistant professor gigs. Before adjunct was what I could get. And now? Not even that.

Like not even once? I pressed. Hitchhiking? My date who became my husband, at least for a while, if I understand his intent by leaving me recently, said *no* in a way that I knew to shut up about it for good.

*

Before he left us, the Portuguese driver tried to kiss me. I bit his lip to stop him. Where had I ripped that idea from? Some movie or book.

He got mad. Pushed me from him and fingered his mouth. Later my friend said, I thought he was going to hit you. Why'd you do that?

She was mad too.

I shrugged her off. What I didn't say was that I'd also thought he was going to hit me. Some memorable story, one for the ages, something I'd thought I could one day tell the kids.

*

Weeks before, immediately after the phone call at night to the hostel in Amsterdam, my friend and I sat on the floor outside our dorm room, nighties tucked around our legs. She'd just learned her grandmother had cancer and might not make it. The fight after fight between the two of them over proprieties, over my friend's vegetarianism and the curly hair she refused to tame, the intransigent fact of the fierce old woman herself—gone? It was weird to think. I nodded. Weird I knew. The previous summer my father had an affair and my mother told me about it and now I told my friend about it. I told her how, when the woman called my mother on the phone to say she was so in love with her husband, my father, my mother told her she was only in love with his credit cards.

My friend put her feet flat on the floor and rocked back against the hallway wall. She laughed her ass off. My god, she gasped. What a stupid cliché.

Even earlier on the trip, before we'd hit the road, we'd stayed in London. At Trafalgar Square my friend undertook a spat with me. Talk to me, she semi-shouted. You literally dumb bitch. You need to tell me what you're thinking, share your thoughts. Otherwise I might as well have left you at home.

The sun is nice today, the sun is too hot. Another beer, why not. Look at that old man over there. In Madrid I chanced telling her I was afraid of becoming one of the numerous homeless some day. You won't, she said airily, you have family, friends. This sun is too hot.

*

What I did once: after her first suicide attempt, when she was in the hospital over March break when we were fifteen, I declined her single working mom's invitation to host me at their house so I could help my friend through this difficult period. Instead I went to Myrtle Beach with my parents and little brother. Every afternoon the sib and I rode The Monster at the sleazy mini-fairgrounds down the street from our efficiency motel room. Every morning we crossed the street to the hotel that actually was on the beach. We baked in the sun by the heated pool and swam. We ran back and forth between the cold ocean and pool, which we jumped in to feel the burn, and I got mild sunstroke on our last day. Somewhere in there, for six bucks in a tourist shop, I bought my friend a pickled octopus jammed into a small jar.

You bet it was dead. Worse, she'd already gone vegetarian. When I got back home, more red and blistered than tanned, I did visit her in the hospital. The look on her face. Her in that huge blue gown, a big bandage around her wrist.

This was before Europe. I had no excuse. It was before my friend told me, that night on the Portuguese beach sitting beside the driver who spoke little to no English, that I really, really did not want to lose my virginity this way. Believe her. She knew all about it, having lost hers that spring, in the sleeping bag she'd borrowed from me so she could go camping with this guy from our history class. He'd been a child actor in popular TV commercials and evolved into a cute teen actor doing same. Not many years later, as a handsome adult he'd become a minor celebrity, acting in a show about a Canadian Mountie and writing screenplays about the Second World War, always assigning himself the tortured hero role.

Were those waves I heard from inside the tent that night in Portugal? Crashing closer, shuffling farther out. It's true we had no idea about the tides.

*

I get up and eat more ice cream standing at the kitchen sink then drop my bowl in. When I met my husband he had a lot of friends. I, as I proudly felt at the time, had few. Some point I was trying to make. About integrity, depth, soul. I hadn't and still haven't spoken to my friend from childhood and teenhood and young adulthood, this ex-friend going on twenty years now.

What's my point? What was even the point of us. That's what I wonder in the shower, thinking about those days when we believed we could make ourselves into who we wanted and that life would bless us in complicated, interesting ways.

At the fridge again I select a frozen dinner. Come on, I urge the microwave. What's your problem? I'm busy. I need to check the wiki for new jobs listings, for news of what I don't have. Requests for better people, sorry, more viable candidates, better fits for precious programs, to send additional materials, to schedule Zoom interviews and campus visits. News of who got what in the end. Slim pickings these days in my field. I'm History, pre-modern. Not exactly a booming business, and I have too much experience for some departments and not enough for others.

I shouldn't kid myself. The problem is I'm old.

I press my head to my table and pretend I'm giving thanks.

I hunch over my phone to scan Insta and Facebook, my new job. Search for signs of my old friend. No trail. I check for her parents even though I already know that her dad died three years ago, according to the online obit. The adult daughter is high up in hospitality, convention centres.

It's true I have no intention of otherwise getting in touch.

Not exactly stalking, I exhume my old friend's brother. Seems he landed on his feet. The fancy archaeology post overseas. The tsunami of co-publications. Frequent international travel to oversee far-flung digs. All this acclaimed expertise at laying bare the the historical record with his Danish professor wife.

His illustrious career. My friend, no trace.

*

After Portugal and Paris we returned to England. We were somewhere I can't remember when she received a letter from her brother, the dirt-digger. Shane, older than her by five years. An art major back home. Since childhood I'd had such a crush on him. Oh, Shane! We must have been somewhere we'd actually planned to be, for her to have received mail. His letter said he had a girlfriend, with a cute Scandi accent. He was writing expressly to let my friend know.

Next thing she was gone. Taking the train north to meet up with him, having instructed me to stay put until she returned and could let me know what's what. Like I even knew what that meant or might mean.

I wandered the quaint streets for two days. For meals I bought glass bottles of milk with the cream on top. I leaned over the railing above a river where sticks rushed by stirring the foam.

A man, middle-aged and trim, approached. I like your colours, he said, pointing to my army pants. He asked me where I was from. He tried to take me to a pub. He told me he was Irish, did I know much about The Troubles?

This was pre-Bobby Sands and very much IRA and terrible violence on both sides, many sides, even I understood that at the time. The man said he liked my hair, near black. And how old was I?

Eventually on a crowded street I dodged him. Crossed paths again and shook my head at my boots. Although I liked my colours too, or thought I did, or didn't know what I thought, he wasn't who I would ever tell any of this to.

My friend returned with not much to say. A new set to her jaw. We took ourselves to sour-smelling pubs for pale ales and packets of crisps. To North Wales and London again, exchanging even fewer words except to point out the stupidity of a young woman at a hostel near Snowdon who'd washed her hair with a bar of laundry soap, so much for her flirting with the handsome young guy from Greece. Or we noted the prevalence of sporting dogs, silky with hauteur, on tony streets. Even their panting pink tongues seemed swish, we declared, swish, trying the word on for size.

*

Does it go without saying? She'd fucked me a few times when we were kids, and a few more times when we were sixteen before giving up on me. Replacing me with that sharp actor guy.

*

In Geneva, where we'd arranged partway through our trip to have money wired, as these were pre- bank machine days, a teller asked for our passports. *Canadienne*, he said. *Français ou anglais?*

We froze. He tipped his head to one side. It was the first time I'd actually heard someone tut-tut. *Anglais*, we managed to get out. *Oui, anglais.*

As if we'd needed a moment to figure at least that one out. As if he did, at that point.

He pushed our cash toward us. *Vive le Québec libre*, he said.

And earlier, we'd crossed the border into Germany and a young woman picked us up and gave us a ride to Cologne and invited us to stay with her and her roommates. She was pretty, a student of Islamic studies, rolled her own cigarettes, came from a typical bourgeois German family, she told us. Understand? Yes, German, we said.

That night, she and her roommates took us to a protest in the city centre. A lawyer friend of theirs spoke on a bullhorn to the crowd. One of the roommates told us as we sat cross-legged on the grass to be ready to run if the police came. One of the roommates' names was Ulrike. Her boyfriend, who also lived in the small basement apartment, was Andreas. They were readying to travel to Afghanistan, they told us. Afghanistan, we said. We'd heard of it. We sort of knew where it was. In that country they'd train. You understand? Yes, we said, we know, train.

*

I'm trying not to get ahead of myself here, but. Before I stopped speaking to my friend she had a baby. We were twenty-two. The baby was born late, giant, scratching itself in the womb and requiring my friend to have an episiotomy and the baby, umbilical cord wrapped around its neck for its first appearance in our world, to be airlifted to a major research hospital and placed in an incubator alongside the high-risk preemies. My poor friend. Stuck in another hospital, in the small burb where she and her clueless-seeming spouse were raising weedy vegetables in a commune and studying social work.

I took the bus from our native city with her mom to visit the baby. Two hours past drab fields under a grey March sky. Her mom had been like a second mother to me when my own was melting down over my father's cheating ways. As the bus bumped along the highway, this good woman asked if I'd never thought it strange how close my friend had been, growing up, to her brother. The one who for years I'd had a massive crush on. Did he like me, did he not, didn't, did. Years of this.

I turned my head away from the streaked window. My friend's mom's face twisted, her eyes searching. I smiled to reassure her. Strange? How do you mean?

*

How had I missed it? Maybe two years after the birth of her daughter, and not long before we said goodbye one night on a downtown street corner, really goodbye, we shared a litre of garbage wine at a noisy café, and at one point she leaned her elbows on the checked tablecloth, her face so familiar to me, more so even than my own, that I knew something was coming, something I wouldn't like. My heart sank. For sure she'd tell me what.

When she did, I remembered her mom's strange question to me.

You must have figured it out ages ago, my friend finished. I mean, big duh.

My friend, her brother: lovers, once upon a time. I imagine my eyes grew round, forehead scrunched. Myself in some movie. How a person should react upon stuff finally falling into place. Cue the close up, strike the bittersweet chords. Imagine me saying, Are you okay? Am I? Who ever is? Questions like car headlights searching amber fields. Or driving on, just passing through. Like me, whose superpower it was, to nod and shrug and gaze into outer space. Coast by.

Then she was on to the actor guy, her undying crush. He was so great. Tim, oh Tim! I needed to give him a chance. I needed a new hairstyle. I should never wear dresses. They made me look like I could easily be knocked down.

Then she had to run. The baby, oh Christ, she needed to get to the daycare and pick her up.

Her life changing in important ways. Not like mine, at that point. Not that she asked about it much.

*

Not that I've ever wanted a baby. Not that she ever asked. But couldn't she have? And if not, why not?

*

My husband was, is, another case. He wanted. Wants.

Leaving me to my confusion with tense.

It's your decision, he told me.

I can't hear you, I said, for only the millionth time.

His knuckles whitened on the grip of his roller case. It's true we've been nomadic, living in this city and that, Cleveland to Oswego to Guelph to Windsor, poised between my previous and my next visiting positions, unbound too by his fortunate ability to work remote.

My husband has never hit me. Never would. Will—should he return. Should I ask him to. Hand out, begging. For him to leave off driving his Corolla all the way to Pullman, Washington. Or continuing on to points further west, escaping my not-calls until salt tides bear him far enough away that he can make peace with us on some strange shore. One I'll likely never know.

I can't hear you. I can't hear you.

He said, Marianne, you never fucking do.

*

I know I'm supposed to move this whole thing forward instead of keeping on going back. Stringing things out while I beg the past for I don't know what, ideas, even a single good one for what comes next. What to do. I am begging you, please. A new you, fresh us that no longer includes someone I might cruelly wish finally dead to me. Please—would that be me, could I be that one? But look. At the zoo in Arnhem, a giraffe ate leaves from a tree, neck stretched over the walkway. Oh, giraffe! As we walked beneath the creature, my friend and I heard the swallow taking the long way down. In Arnhem we drank beer and studied our maps. Where we might go. Auto-stop, that's how we'd get around. That's how we did. It's not so, it wasn't, so complicated. Auto-stop.

DOWNSIZING

Colette Maitland

"And where are we off to now?"

We?

Ignoring her bloody highness, Curt liberates his peacoat from one of two dozen black faux-velvet clothes hangers—Babe's 'must have' purchase when she and Curt last drifted through Walmart. Two jackets permitted each season in the apartment's coffin-like front hall cupboard, Babe decreeing so on move-in day before staking claim to the closet's lower half for her individually boxed snow globe collection; yet for some reason she's slid two dozen hangers across a metal bar barely capable of accommodating them, imagining what, Des appearing in the dead of winter with twenty-one of her best friends?

"I *said*, where're you off to?" Babe, presiding now over the kitchen table with her scissors, glue stick and scrapbook, local newspaper splayed to the obits: reaping the dead, her mid-week morning ritual.

With difficulty, Curt half-shutters the closet's bifold door, its refusal to accede an ongoing irritant since he and Babe took possession of the apartment last summer. Easy fix *if* he still possessed a screwdriver, a hammer, and an adjustable wrench.

"Curt?"

He's been after Babe to contact Lorne Stuckle, the building's super. Babe, who donated all of Curt's tools to the curb in a cardboard box marked "D" for diabetes weeks into their new living arrangement while, for a few hours, he'd escaped their meagre square footage, volunteering to stock shelves at the food bank. Damned if Curt will ring the man, but apparently preserving obits, knitting, that true crime book club of hers, *Ellen* and *The View*, not to mention whatever she and her shrill coven of widowed girlfriends might conjure up in the course of a day take precedence over a stubborn bifold door.

"Curt!"

"I heard you," he says, pleasantly enough. Removing cap and driving gloves from the sleeve of his coat, he silently slips them on.

"So answer already!"

Boots next, careful not to disrupt Babe's footwear so she's nothing to criticize upon his return.

Somewhere in his wife's brain a filament warms.

"It's the bankers box, isn't it? You're," finger jab, "*still*," finger jab, "mad!"

Finger pointing, a sure sign his current demeanour's chafing Babe's thin skin. Jingling car keys in his coat pocket because she detests when he does so, and without raising his voice he confirms her hunch, "Yes. Still."

Babe's incredulous blue eyes frost over, her cheaters toboggan to the tip of her nose. "Honestly, you can be such a child, sometimes."

"Better a child than a Grade A bitch." Mouthed bitterly behind her back on occasion though never to her face until now, and delivered with equanimity, Curt notes with satisfaction how 'bitch' has momentarily disabled Babe's speech centre. Best to make a swift exit.

Stepping into the low-lit carpeted hallway, Curt quietly latches the door, itching to rock it off its hinges the way he used to when they owned the house. Now? Neighbours to the left, right, below, above—childhood friends, ex-customers from his butcher shop days, even an old fling, one Babe and her gal pals didn't sniff out—Mable, summer '93. Thin walls, loose lips; retirees, men and women alike with nothing better to do than get the goods on each other, spread it about like a social disease as they forestall the inevitable transition from independent living to nursing home. He hates the apartment lifestyle, no point sugar-coating it. Never in his seventy-four years did he envision a scenario where he'd be plodding the length of an apartment hall, neighbours' doors decked out in drek for all occasions, stopping to engage in meaningless chit-chat with whoever happened to be exiting the building the same moment as he. Case in point, the latest occupant of #201, located beside the stairwell. Sleek white hair, dangly earrings, puffy red winter coat—she trails a tiny, leashed, dewy-eyed pooch, sporting a miniature replica of the self-same jacket.

"Good morning," she says, her voice a throaty pleasure.

"Yes, hello."

"Out for a walk?"

"No, no, running an errand." Ever the gentleman, he opens the door, waits, his reward a pleasant whiff of something as she slips past.

"Susan Poulson," offering a gloved hand, "I'm new."

Name familiar, bio too, Babe all over that—moved in last month, widow, Calgary transplant relocating to be closer to a daughter, two grandkids, nine and seven; nice enough, tries too hard.

"Curt," he says. "I'm old," which scores him a smile, a laugh. Pretty in her day, he imagines, attractive still, great cheek-bones, a sense of humour too, makes him want to linger in the stairwell. "We moved in seven months ago." Seven months, one week, three tedious days.

"How do you like it?"

"It's been," hell, "an adjustment, for me especially. My wife loves it. You've met her. Babe?"

"Babe. Yes." Doing her best to stifle what Curt interprets as a 'poor bugger look,' she bends to scoop up her dog. "Well, I'd better get Rosie downstairs before she bursts."

"Of course. What sort of dog is she?" He doesn't care, only wants to keep air in the conversation until they reach ground level.

"Terripoo."

"Terri *what*?"

"Poo—a terrier-slash-miniature poodle—mixed breed, glorified mutt, take your pick. I paid too much for the little fart, but she's wonderful company. Aren't you, Rosie?"

"I'm sure. Well," opening wide the outside door, "enjoy this wintry day."

"Yes, you too."

"Spring will be here before we know it."

Lifting a gloved hand in response to what she's certain to have recognized as the bullshit pleasantry it is, she and her furball pick their way west toward the woods and walking path, leaving Curt to assess the sorry state of their building's parking lot—snowbanks clinging to the lot's edges, left to melt as daylight temperatures climb, causing tiny tributaries to trickle across the pavement, water which then freezes as the sun and mercury drop. No crystal ball required for him to predict a broken hip here, a cracked ankle there before spring. At the very least, Stuckle should be out after sun-up with a bag of road salt. Last month Curt created a petition, circulating it amongst the other tenants before bypassing Stuckle, handing it off to a member of the board. Mount Olympus has yet to weigh in, but Stuckle did recently assign Curt a new parking spot far from the building's main entrance; a tenant with mobility issues requiring his space. *You of all people will understand.* Another reason Curt's leaving the cupboard door issue to Babe. If this lot were his responsibility it'd be bare and dry, by God, like he kept his own driveway come winter.

Nostalgia swoops down, pecks at Curt as he plots his way to the Buick, for the driveway, the house, the land, the quiet most of all. Babe never embracing country life but loving him enough at time of purchase to accept it, until the business with Maggie Thompson, after which Babe took to the spare room for good. *The last straw, you cheating bastard*. Meaning it this time, ushering in the cold war phase of their marriage; the house, land and locale her soft targets. She began with the bullfrogs—their sex-crazed racket had driven Babe batty each spring and summer for twenty years. How much longer did he expect her to suffer it? Living so far from neighbours, she fretted over break-ins, picturing Curt and her hog-tied, throats slit, shot to death like the Clutter family in *In Cold Blood*. Oh, how she pined for real pizza, delivered hot and gooey to the door. The frozen kind didn't hold a candle, not even real food, the Twinkie of entrees. She missed the old letter carrier from town; their inane conversations broke up her day. How many more times would she have to risk life and limb crossing the highway to pluck flyers and bills from the mailbox?

"Move out, if you don't like it," he'd counter, and she'd huff and puff, place a lengthy call to Des wherever she happened to be living at the time. Babe hadn't worked in years—thank-you, fibromyalgia—possessed little money of her own, didn't hold with divorce. A good thing too because she'd be entitled to half of everything he'd worked so hard to acquire. Where else did she have to go? He'd outlive her roll call of ailments—diabetes, high blood pressure and cholesterol, the aforementioned fibromyalgia—Curt's genes more robust, his father outlasting Mother by nearly fifteen years. So, no one was more surprised than Curt by his heart attack and ensuing emergency bypass; Babe hovering over his hospital bed, tearfully triumphant as if five of six lottery ticket numbers had appeared. Who'd cut the grass now, she demanded first of him and then Des. Who'd clean out the eavestroughs, rake the leaves, shovel come winter? How would she manage, God forbid, if he went before she did?

God forbid. His dear wife, so eager to cut and paste Curt's obit into that damned scrapbook of hers, he could almost hear the measured snips of her scissors.

South west of Curt's belt buckle, James Brown and a chorus of horns get down—*I feel good, da-na-na-na-na-na-na.* The ring tone Des downloaded onto his phone last month when, on her way from Toronto to Ottawa for a conference, she blew in for a quick visit, something cheery to combat Curt's winter doldrums. It's her, his best girl.

"Des, hey! Listen, I'm in the parking lot, steps from the car. Hang on a sec?"

"Certainly." *Certainly,* not 'sure' or 'yup'—at work, of course—clinic day, if he's not mistaken. Her professional tone still a thrill to his ear—his daughter, The Cardiologist. Tucking the phone into his shirt pocket for safekeeping, he crosses the last few yards wondering: can Des hear his heart? Is she counting the beats right now, monitoring him for signs of new disease?

"Could you hear it?" He asks, once settled. "My ticker," he adds, when she doesn't immediately respond, "I popped the phone into my shirt pocket. Lot's icy; don't need to shatter the screen along with my hip when I go down."

"No, Dad, I couldn't. Just heard an earful from Mom, though."

"Yeah. I figured."

"You called her a bitch? Stormed out of the apartment?"

"I did not *storm.* Is that what she's saying, because I promise you, I was a *mouse.* Did she happen to mention *why* I called her that?"

"No. I couldn't make out half of what she said with all the crying and whatnot. She thinks you've left her."

"What?"

"That. You've. Left her. For good."

Damn. That's hardball. Babe: 1. Curt: 0.

"Are you? Leaving her? 'Cause maybe it'd be…"

"Of course not!"

"…for the best…"

"I'm on my way to the drugstore."

"…before one of you kills the other."

"To buy her a birthday card." There. Let that sink in. "Still coming to the party Saturday?"

"Dunno, it still on?"

"Absolutely! Event room's booked. I've ordered a cake from Metro, cheese tray, veggie platter too, invited friends from the apartment complex." Not the Poulson woman, though maybe now they've met he should, even if she does try too hard. "Your aunt's even RSVP'd."

"I thought Ida and Mom weren't speaking."

"Tempest in a teapot, you know what they're like. Besides, your mother only turns seventy once. Ida's capable of remaining civil for an afternoon especially when free food's on offer. You're still bringing balloons?"

"Yes?"

Ha! Busted! Bet she's reaching for pen and paper right now, scrawling BALLOONS.

"Anything else?"

"Pop. And how about some of those lemon squares you make, for people not fond of cake."

"People like you?"

"Yes."

"Deal. But you'll need to do something for me. Apologize to Mom."

Of course, why she's calling in the middle of a busy morning. "It's your mother who should apologize. She threw out my bankers box."

"It doesn't mat—wait, *the* bankers box?"

"Kicked to the curb like she did my tools, my *National Geographic* collection and, need I remind you, most of my books." He *thinks* she kicked it to the curb, she hasn't actually said. "Like she'd do to me if she could," he adds, hoping to secure

Des's sympathy once and for all in case Babe phones her back with some other tale of woe.

"Dad, that's, wow, that's *terrible*."

"And *now* you see why I called her what I called her." Curt: 1. Babe: 1.

"I do. I *do*, but Dad, two wrongs don't make a right. You used to say that all the time."

"No I didn't."

"Sure you did, when I was a bratty teenager and Mom and I'd fight."

"I don't ever recall employing that expression." A giggle/ snort, is she five or nearly fifty? For a moment he feels young again. Relevant. "Not once."

"Stop."

"Stop what?"

"Making me laugh, this is serious. You two are living in a nine-hundred-square-foot-two-bedroom box."

"Nine-thirty-five if you count the bathroom," and he does since it's the only space Babe won't charge into, "which you and your mother thought a great idea after my heart attack and surgery. Ganging up on me, taking advantage of my weakened state. I've forgiven you, sweetheart, but I have *not* forgotten."

Weary sigh. "Look, my patients are waiting. Can you *please* take the high road, here?"

In the distance, Susan Poulson and pooch, back so soon?

"Dad?"

"Yes, high road." Appears to be favouring her right side. "Am programming it into my GPS as we speak."

"Hardy-har-har. Gotta go. Love you."

"Love you right back. Bye."

Foot, knee or hip, one's out of kilter. Returning the phone to his shirt pocket, he exits the car, makes his way toward her.

"I couldn't help notice the limp, are you okay?"

"I'm fine. Embarrassed more than anything. Slipped in the woods, landed on my keester! Tore a hole in my coat." Executing an awkward, painful pirouette to show him. "After ordering Rosie's mini-me coat, too. Thing cost a fortune. Blasted internet."

"Yes, well. Are you sure? I'm heading downtown, be happy to drop you at the clinic."

"Kind of you to offer, Curt, but it's nothing a couple of extra-strength Tylenol and a heating pad won't handle."

"What about the stairs? Here," reaching for the dog, "why don't I. . ." Curt's innocent overture is met by a snarling snap, "Oh!"

"Rosie! *Bad girl*! She didn't bite, did she?"

"No, no. I'm surprised though, dogs generally like me."

"She's very protective, I should've warned you."

"Well," hands raised, "consider me warned," backing away from Rosie's still-bared teeth and her deluded mistress, glad now he didn't extend a party invite. "And do take care of your, uh, issue."

*

Each New Year's Day, once Babe had packed her ornaments into a Rubbermaid tub and directed Curt to both hump the Christmas tree to the highway's edge for pick-up and retrieve the outdoor lights so Babe could store them in a second Rubbermaid tub, after she'd removed all fake pine boughs and twinkle lights from the interior windowsills and door frames, filling to capacity two large green garbage bags, boxed up her Christmas-themed snow globes, Santa figurines and angels, bade adieu to her seasonal pillows, napkins, dishes, tablecloths and throws, she'd disappear into their bedroom for a time to sort through her closet, reappearing with a fully stocked knitting basket—yarn, needles, dog-eared pattern booklets. Babe's post-holiday mission, manufacturing infant layettes to hawk at the following November's Christmas craft fair or, as Curt referred to it, the Christmas *crap* fair; each set consisting of a pair of thumb-less mittens, a hat, a sweater, but no booties—modern moms preferred tiny socks sold three to a pack, booties a waste of wool, Babe's time. Powder pink, baby blue, lemon yellow, mint green, one or two sets a week, depending on each pattern's complexity, severity of her carpal tunnel symptoms. Halting production only during the dog days of August when a single strand of yarn brushing against her upper thigh inspired sweat to fringe her forehead. She'd sell enough layettes to justify the Christmas craft fair fee, purchase a few gifts, fund her wool basket for the following year, but never enough to pay off the credit card or cover a mortgage payment. A hobby, not a job, no matter what she argued when it came time for Curt and her to review their finances.

Des must've been thirteen, fourteen when Babe attempted to groom her. Curt and Babe still shared the master bedroom back then, but they hadn't fucked in months, Babe punishing him for some indiscretion or other, doesn't matter now, but at the time? Heightened tensions, arguments over nothing, periods of silence, Des caught in the middle, not then privy to the particulars. Teaching Des to knit, Curt came to understand, Babe's way of reaching out, holding on. Curt? He connected with Des weekday mornings as he drove them into town, dropping her at school on his way to the butcher shop, no Babe to muck up the works. Sports, boys, teachers, classes, assignments, parties, drugs, abortion, politics, nothing off limits; they laughed a lot. Des told him, years later, *I could say anything, an-y-thing, and you'd never freak out.* For a time that winter, she vented over Babe's knitting 'crusade'—*Each afternoon I come in from the bus and there she is, waving half a sweater in my face, or a hat, so I try to be like, 'oh, cool,' 'cause obviously it means a lot to her and I don't want to hurt her feelings, right? But then she says, 'sit and I'll show you how,' and I'm like, 'fuuuuck,' so I make up an excuse like, 'Mom, I would only I have this project to finish or this test to study for,' but sometimes she looks so bummed when I play the homework card I can't deal, so I sit down and she hands me THE fattest set of needles* she owns, like needles for dummies, right? But it's no use. 'Cause literally? My eyebrows have a better chance of knitting together. Knitting #101 arising as a topic between the three of them only once, at the dinner table:

Mom tried to show me how to knit again.

Oh?

Yeah, for like, the umpteenth time.

Babe to Des: *You said you were bored . . .*

Not that bored, Mom.

So sue me, but first, eat your turnip.

I hate turnip—mashed, buttered, sugared, it still tastes like crap. And what would be the point of suing, YOU have no money.

Babe to Curt: *See?*

See what?

The way you undermine me with my own daughter!

How is any of this my fault? To Des: *Come to the shop on Saturday, run the front cash, help with the deli counter. See what real work looks like.*

Hot, rather than scalding, the black tea Babe threw in his face, staining his favourite shirt.

Mom! Jeez! Don't be such a frickin' psycho!

Make your own damn meals from now on!

Three days of peanut butter and jam, canned soup, pork and beans before Curt capitulated: *The way I see it, we apologize or learn how to cook.*

No way, Dad, I bought you that shirt for Christmas!

True, but you, we, were disrespectful, and Des, two wrongs don't make a right.

There it is, of course, why Curt's brain is dredging up that long-ago ruckus now, while he vacantly stares at Pharmasave's Cards-for-all-Occasions wall. Two wrongs, yada-yada. This sort of reverie occurring more often, it seems, since his heart attack, a post-surgical by-product? He'll ask Des, Saturday, if she can spare five minutes of private time, but for now, old man, focus. Bridal shower cards, wedding cards, anniversary cards, cards for baby showers, baptisms, confirmations, graduations, Valentine's Day, St. Paddy's Day; get-better-soon cards, bereavement cards, where do they hide the bloody birthday cards?

"To your left, sir. They have their own display."

"Oh! Thank you," a glance at her name tag, "Jen, how could I have missed it right there in front of my face," and then sotto voce, "I said that last bit out loud, didn't I?"

"Affirmative," matching whisper for whisper. He likes this girl, her little gold-hooped nostril, shoulder-length burgundy hair and snow-white skin; squared shoulders too, and a straight spine, no slouching. She'd be a granddaughter's age if Des had ever produced one. It's a weekday morning, what's she doing here?

"Shouldn't you be in school, young lady?"

"I am, this is a work placement, I'm earning a credit, deciding if pharmacy is for me."

"Work placement, eh? That's a thing?"

"It is! Now, can I help you with anything else?"

"Well," thinking there are worse ways to spend part of his day, "the card *is* for my wife and she's a hard woman to please. Can you spare a moment?"

A ten-minute charm offensive choosing a card with the aid of his chatty fantasy granddaughter, followed by his weekly two-hour volunteer stint at the Humane Society, a trip to Canadian Tire to purchase a five-kilogram bag of road salt, soup and sandwich at the bakery, then it's back to the apartment parking lot to forge a salt trail from his parking spot to the sidewalk and back again. The other tenants can look after themselves, or conscript a resentful child, grandchild; since Des is both based in Toronto and unapologetically single, he and Babe are on their own. *Your fault*—Des, ten years ago, when they'd called to wish her a happy 40th and, like every

birthday since Des hit her late-twenties, Babe brought it up—
*What about marriage, kids? We're not getting any younger, you
know.*

You two didn't make marriage look like much fun.

Fair enough.

Babe not quite so understanding once the phone call
ended: *Did you HEAR her? 'You two,' YOU FUCKING TWO!
Our marriage would've been fine if somebody* (finger jab)
could've kept (finger jab) *his DICK* (finger jab) *in check. . . . She
knows about your women. Oh, yes, yes indeed. Had a heart-to-
heart with our Des before she lit out for university; she couldn't
leave fast enough. I hoped she'd seen the real you, but no, she's
STILL Daddy's little girl. Makes me sick.*

Not nearly sick enough.

Stowing the remaining salt in his trunk, Curt comes round
to the passenger side of the car with the intent of plucking
Babe's birthday card from the seat when he smacks into an all-
too-familiar wall of fatigue—another heart surgery by-product which thankfully occurs less often now than in those first
six months. Nothing to do but drop into the passenger seat,
close his eyes, wait it out, hope nobody takes him for dead.

Sketches—in that bankers box. Pencil mostly, a few ren-
dered in ink. He'd always drawn as a kid, sketching this and
that, but only became serious about it in high school; a way
to impress his art teacher—the lovely Ms. Lyon—subject of
many a late-night jerk-off session until his acne cleared and he
discovered girls his own age. He stopped drawing altogether
after graduation. None of his early work survived Mother's
cleaning binges, his fecklessness.

The bankers box 'period' kicked off summer of '93, at a
Midway motel room out on #2—a quick study of Mable Con-
nor on a scrap of notepad paper with a ballpoint pen. Mable,
naked, half-draped by a sheet after a 'proper fuck'—her words,
not his. Curt can't recall what caused him to reach for pad and
pen, but Mable's hoot of delight when she recognized herself

fed something deep down. He gave her the drawing, certainly couldn't bring it home. But later that week he purchased a sketchpad and pencils, stashing them in the glove compartment of his truck. He began pulling off to the road's edge to draw whatever caught his eye between work and home—birds, trees, livestock, wildflowers, barns, fence posts—continuing even after Mable called it quits. He stopped in '95—no reason he can think of, but he kept the sketchpads, purchased the bankers box. Hasn't flipped through those sketches since before the house sold when, in an unguarded moment, he suggested to Babe maybe they frame a couple to display in the new apartment. *Fancy yourself a bit of a Picasso do you, Curt?* Laughing her way into the kitchen to poke at a meatloaf in the oven.

Bitch.

'Your women.' Four, all told; Babe only aware of three, so three. Not the best record, nor the worst. He always came home didn't he? Always provided. Never blamed Babe. Mismatched libidos. No one's fault.

Feeling somewhat recharged, Curt opens his eyes. Consults his watch—3 p.m. Dinner at 5:30, if Babe still plans to feed him. Meals and early evening the best part of their time together—she's still a fine cook and they both enjoy eating at TV tables while sparring over *Jeopardy.* Maybe he'll discover Babe crumpled on the kitchen floor—dead of a stroke, of choking on her own venom—*what's known as 'comeuppance,' Alex. Now, let's try "Just Desserts" for $800.*

Two hours and change, enough time to wander through the building collecting birthday card well wishes and signatures for his wife of forty-nine years. Can't stop playing the part now, not with the end so near.

A tactical error, calling her that, not how a gentleman behaves. Dollars to donuts Babe didn't stop with Des. She'll have visited Agnes, Fern and Barb's apartments in the interim. He'll leave those cold-eyed harpies till last, but first, why not a friendly face? Why not pay Mable a visit? He hasn't caught sight of her in months; Babe says that's because she's gone off, can't keep anyone, anything straight. Only leaves her apartment now in the company of her son. But Mable will recognize Curt, of course she will. And even if she doesn't, he has to know, does she still have it; does she still have that sketch?

THE ONES WE CARRY WITH US

Sara O'Leary

A few years ago, I accidentally midwifed a death. The woman was elderly and had lived alone for many years, and her death should not have been unexpected. But it came as a shock to me. The woman's name was Agatha, but she told me once that she had another name given to her by her grandfather because hers was an old family name and it had already belonged to too many people.

At Agatha's funeral, I learned what her secret name was, and it made me sad because the whole time she was dying, I was calling her name. She was getting further and further away, and it wasn't that I thought she would come back just that I wanted her to know I was still there. But the whole time I was calling her by the name that was already all worn out by the time it reached her.

*

For a while, I volunteered at a senior's day centre where most of the clients had dementia. I became very fond of a woman named Marjorie, who was in her nineties but who was also more alive than most people I know. Marjorie was convinced that we'd been schoolmates. "Chummed around together" was how she put it. I'd get her to tell me stories and then the next time I saw her I could remind her of things we had done together when we were both at boarding school in Rothesay, New Brunswick. Sometimes we would talk about what it was like being at McGill just after the war. The larks we got up to. It was all lies, of course. But it was also true.

*

There's a story I've never quite been able to tell. It was about something that happened to me one Halloween when I was in my twenties. We lived at that time in a haunted house, but this story is not about that. Our apartment was part of a building of row houses that opened right onto the sidewalk of Milton Street in Montreal. During the day, if you sat in our living room, you could listen to the conversations of passersby, a thing I used to do that proves I knew how to waste time even before we had the internet.

But this was nighttime. I was alone because I'd decided not to go to the Halloween party that night. I didn't like Halloween, and I wasn't crazy about parties. There were too many parties in those days. I stayed home, and I probably read a book because we didn't own a television and there was, as I said, no internet. I have a picture of myself from that time standing in front of our bookcase, so it's possible I could even work out what book I was reading. It might have been *Nightwood*, as those were my Djuna Barnes years. It could have been a book I loved at the time called *That Kind of Woman*. It's extraordinary to me that, in those days, all the books we owned fit into one bookcase. And that it still felt like untold riches.

There I was, in the living room of our apartment that was practically right on the sidewalk, when there was a knock at the door. A loud, frantic knock. I went and opened the door. Did I think it was someone I knew? Did I just open my door to anyone in those days? Yes, probably.

It was a young woman, roughly my age, but much, much smaller. Shaking, cold, frightened. "Help me," she said, and so I let her in and closed the door behind her.

She said her boyfriend was chasing her. That she was frightened. That she wanted to call her mother to come and get her. Could she use my phone?

I watched her dial, listened to her talk. "Yes, again," she said. "I know," she said. "Milton Street," she said. And then she hung up.

She asked me for a glass of water, and I went out to the kitchen to get it for her. The kitchen was my favourite part of that apartment. I stood there for a moment, letting the water run. I knew there was something wrong with her story. I knew something was wrong. I didn't know how it was going to end.

*

I had no idea that police always had to come out in the event of a sudden death at home. When my friend Agatha died, I first called my husband and asked him to call 911. I had to open the door to the first responders, who turned out to be our local fire brigade, and then the paramedics, and then the police. It was a very small apartment and it filled quickly. I kept having to explain who I was. Not a granddaughter. Not an employee or a care worker. A friend.

The police officer and I had been operating at cross-purposes with my poor French and his poor English, so when he asked me if he could read what I write it seemed a bit of a non sequitur. Flustered already, I grew more flustered and told him that I had a review in that weekend's *Globe and Mail* that he could read. He shook his head at me impatiently. "No, no," he said (*non, non*). "Can I read your *hand*writing?"

He then gave me a pen and paper (looking back, I see something like the exam booklets we hand out to students), and I wrote my statement. When you are writing fiction, it is as much about what you leave out as what you leave in. Writing a police statement seemed much the same. I kept wondering what it was that they were looking for. Evidence that her death was somehow my responsibility? It felt that way.

I wrote that I had made her breakfast shortly before she died. That I had to insist because she was so weak and I was worried that she hadn't been eating in the days prior, which she had spent locked away in her apartment with what she told me was a cold. That she finally agreed to a boiled egg, but then stood over me as I leaned into the fridge and, when I opened the carton of farm eggs and instinctively chose the largest one, she put out her hand to stay mine. "I'm saving that one for someone," she said.

*

I used to have a newspaper column. When my son was small, he opened the paper one time and looked at my little head-shot there and said, "Why is your picture in the paper every week when you aren't even famous?"

Writing book reviews for the newspaper every week is exactly the sort of job I would have dreamed of in high school if I could have even dreamed of such a thing. I worked from home and, practically daily, books would be delivered to my door. As if things couldn't get any better, I then got a similar job but for radio instead of print. Every week I would be interviewed by the hosts of the afternoon show about a different book. I wrote both their questions and my answers, and we worked from that script. Sometimes I would begin my answers with the phrase "funny you should ask that" because it amused me.

I think I'd do a lot better in life if I could always write both the questions and the answers. All my life I have been both-ered by the question of whether things happen for a reason. I try to imagine myself scripting a response to that, but all I hear is silence.

Once, I heard my young son and his friend quietly con-versing as I walked behind them through a forest on a perfect sunny day.

"I don't want to die," my son said.

"I know," said the other boy. "But we have to."

*

Sometimes my friend Marjorie—friend of my fictional youth—would move forward in time and begin to worry about where her husband was. She would anxiously scan the faces in the room, looking for the one she knew best. She would imagine that we were all at a party together and if she was there then he must be, too. Sometimes, she would turn her chair so that she could see the door in case he entered there. "I hope he hasn't forgotten me," she would say. He'd died years earlier, but I would always reassure her by saying he was on his way. "Of course, he hasn't forgotten you," I would say. "He called. He told me he would be here soon."

As a child I was taught that lying was the worst thing you could do. I was taught to tell the truth. Only later would I learn that sometimes you have to tell it slant.

*

That Halloween night on Milton Street, I returned from the kitchen with the glass of water to find the young woman was shaking even harder than before. She said she would go out to the corner to wait for her mother. She said she would be fine. I didn't want to let her go and I didn't want her to stay. Just before I turned the deadbolt on the door, she took my hand and looked me in the eyes. "You're a good person," she said.

I think about that all the time. Am I?

When I called the police (and this was the first time in my life I'd ever had to do that), they told me that I was not the only one in my neighbourhood who had been conned. They said they would let me know if they recovered my wallet, but not to get my hopes up.

When that girl told me her story, I knew it didn't ring true. I knew there was a lie in it somewhere. But what I didn't know, and what I still don't know, is why she said what she did. I don't know if she really did think I was a good person. I don't know why I care.

*

Here's the thing I now know about dying. It looks like almost anything else. It looks like sitting down to eat an egg. It looks like resting for a moment. It looks like just slowing down. The difference between the slowing down and the stopping is nothing at all.

At Agatha's funeral, people I didn't know would come up to talk to me about the fact that I happened to be there with her when she died. Somehow everyone seemed to know this about me, which was unsettling. "Things happen for a reason," they kept saying. Agatha had believed that her dead son had sent me to be with her, but I didn't see how that could be true.

My friend Marjorie couldn't remember the death of her husband, while my friend Agatha couldn't forget the death of her son. She'd been abandoned by her husband and her son was everything to her. Then, when he was twenty-one, he died. And even though he was gone, she never stopped being his mother. I can't even imagine being in the world that long after your child has left it. Wouldn't it be a kindness to be able to forget certain things had happened?

I used to think that the fear we have of dying was tied to the fear of being forgotten. But now, I think that what we're really afraid of is the ones we love being forgotten. The ones we have both lost and carry with us. I only knew Agatha for a very short time at the end of her long life. But before I left her empty apartment that day, I picked up a photo of her son, which she had left out, meaning to show me when I visited, and I took it with me.

COLLAPSE

Jasmine Sealy

Patrice Martin was hunting in Ganthier, one-hour's drive east of Port-au-Prince, when he collapsed onto the rocky earth. He brought his hand to his chest, squeezed his eyes shut and rolled onto his back. He took three ragged breaths and then let out as loud a yell as he could manage. The sound, high and wheezing, was swept up in the reddish dust of the plains, and carried off. He tried again, but this time no sound came out.

The sun was beginning to set, the sky already dusted with stars. As the light faded, Patrice tried to keep himself conscious by searching for familiar constellations. Next year, his sons would be old enough to hunt and he was already teaching them how to navigate by the night sky, just as his father had taught him. The farther north you travel, the higher Polaris looks in the sky. If the moon is new, connect the tips of the crescent and follow that line down to the horizon, that's south. He ran his fingers through the dirt at his side, grasping at the sparse roots. He closed his eyes.

Patrice's cousin, Arnold, who was also his best friend, was nearby but out of sight, tracking a flock of guinea fowl across the dry, treeless expanse of what was once a virgin mahogany

141

forest. The birds had taken cover in the brush, all except for one, which remained out in the open, pecking at the clayish dirt, its black and white wings splayed. Arnold kept it in his sight, edging forward at a crouch. A cry echoed across the valley and the bird took flight. Arnold raised his head and looked for the source of the sound. Likely the shrill call of a red-tailed hawk. By the time he looked back through his scope, the guinea fowl was gone.

"*Tonère*," he mumbled, rising to go in search of his cousin. He walked slowly, the craggy grasslands uneven beneath his feet. In the distance, Lake Azuie shone blue, its shores dotted with cactus and brambles. Just across the border, in the Dominican Republic, at the same latitude, the forests grew thick and lush in a protected park. An aerial view of the two countries showed the border clearly: dark green giving way to brown. The history of a single island, divided. Arnold couldn't bring himself to hate his neighbour though, they had both been pillaged, their lands plundered, the only difference between them the shape and depth of the scars that remained. Patrice would not agree. "*Se yo ki fucking colon yo kounyean*," he would say. They're the fucking colonizers now.

Arnold reached his truck without running into his cousin. He would later learn he had walked within twenty metres of where Patrice lay silent, alive, but barely. Arnold climbed into the truck and started the engine, his sweat drying in the AC. He fiddled with the radio but could not find a signal. His phone, too, was out of range. Bored, he put his seat back as far he could, and closed his eyes. When he woke, close to an hour later, he groaned. The sun had set, and they had a long drive back to Port-au-Prince, which would now have to be done in the dark. Just a week before, Arnold's childhood friend had been kidnapped on that same road. He had been rescued, unharmed, that same day. But still, it was an inconvenience and expense Arnold wished to avoid. He went in search of his cousin once more.

He found him after almost an hour of searching. Arnold fell to his knees beside Patrice, rolling him onto his back. The temperature had dropped and Patrice's skin was cold. But he had a pulse, and this is what Arnold repeated to himself, over and over, as he carried his cousin to the truck. Arnold was the smaller of the two, short and wiry, kept trim by CrossFit and yoga. Patrice was big. He dressed as Père Noël every year for their extended family Christmas dinner. His youngest son, Alex, was still small enough to crawl up his round belly and rub the bald patch at the top of his skull. "*Pour la chance*," he liked to say. Arnold had to stop every few feet to put his cousin down. Once, with the car in sight, he tripped, and Patrice landed on top of him. Trapped beneath his dying cousin, whose breath was still warm against his cheek, Arnold cried. His tears carried the dust on his cheeks into his mouth. He screamed for help, but there was no one around. He heaved his cousin off his chest and, mumbling apologies through his tears, dragged him by his ankles the rest of the way.

He drove as fast as he dared. The road fell away in places, the wheels of his truck skirting the edges of potholes that would be impossible to get out of without a tow. When they reached Croix des Bouquets the traffic became impassible, cars choking the narrow streets. Arnold lay on his horn, his head out the window, his cries lost to the din. In the backseat Patrice stirred, moaning softly, his eyes fluttering awake. "*Ou anfom kouzen*," Arnold whispered. You're okay, cousin. By the time they made it to the only hospital still open, Hôpital de la Communauté, Patrice was dead.

Later, sitting on a wooden bench outside the emergency room, Arnold called his aunt, Patrice's mother. She spoke loudly, the TV blaring a soap opera in the background. It took several attempts at an explanation before he could bring her to understand what had happened. Once she did, she shrieked, a sound not unlike that a guinea fowl makes when you pierce it somewhere other than the heart. She must have dropped the phone, because the noise grew distant. Arnold hung up, took several breaths, and then called Patrice's wife, Vanessa. The line was busy.

He would later learn his aunt had already called her. Vanessa had been washing dishes at the time, and like her mother-in-law, dropped her phone at the news. It sank into the greasy, sudsy water where it lay for the next four days, until the morning of the funeral, when the dishes were washed by another aunt. After this call, Patrice's mother placed another, to her youngest son, Xavier, who was attending university in Sainte-Foy, Quebec.

Xavier learned of his brother's heart attack at a bar, his arm around a pretty girl from Saguenay he'd been chatting up all evening. He nearly didn't answer his phone, his mother called him too often, but he thought it would impress the girl to hear him speak his native tongue. When he learned of his brother's death, he stumbled off his bar stool and out into the frozen night. He fell to the snow and stayed there, until the girl arrived with his friends in tow, and pulled him to his feet. Later, in his dorm room, he made several calls, one of which was to his cousin, Sebastian, in Montreal. Sebastian then called another cousin, who called another, until eventually, by then the next day, the news reached Olivier, Patrice's second cousin once removed, in Vancouver, BC.

Olivier was watching premiere league football on the couch while his girlfriend, Caroline, read a book on the patio. She sat with her feet up on a plant pot, her chair pushed to the farthest corner of the patio to catch the last sliver of sunlight before it dipped behind the building across from theirs. Olivier hung up the phone, taking in the news. He hadn't seen Patrice in years, not since the last time a cousin's wedding had reunited them in Port-au-Prince.

Olivier tried to remember how old Patrice was. No more than forty-five, surely. He had two young children whose names Olivier also could not recall, though he knew their faces from Instagram. Patrice was well-liked in the family, a big jolly guy, always quick to tell a joke, quicker still to laugh at one. He was the kind of guy who knew a little about a lot of things. Always stirring up trouble, inciting debate, telling dirty jokes that embarrassed the *granmoun*. Olivier felt his loss sharply, a familiar ache. It hurt to think of Haiti, to think of family far away, and Patrice's death drew his attention to that ever-present pain, like pulling a muscle already weakened from previous injury. He glanced at Caroline. Only her legs were visible through the screen door. He considered not telling her about Patrice. Her mood had been restless that day, and he wasn't sure there was anything she could say that would make him feel better. Eventually though, his pain coalesced into something he could name. This was loneliness, he realized. So, after a few more minutes he said, "Babe. My cousin in Haiti died."

She didn't react right away, stopping first to pick her bookmark up from where it had fallen by her feet. She came in, and knelt on the carpet in front of where he sat on the couch, sidling up between his legs. She brought a hand to his cheek. "I'm so sorry, baby. What happened?"

"He had a heart attack while hunting. He was so young. In his forties."

"How horrible." She pulled him in for a hug, and he let his chin rest on her shoulder, breathing in the scent of her. She smelled like cigarette smoke, and faintly of the shampoo they both used. "Which cousin was it?" she asked quietly.

"Patrice."

"Oh . . . Jacqueline's husband?"

"No, that's a different Patrice. This one lives . . . lived in Haiti. He was my second cousin."

"Were you close?"

Olivier pulled out of the embrace, settling back on the couch. Caroline rose and went to the kitchen. "We grew up on the same street," Olivier said, "he was older. I know his younger brother better. But we all used to spend time together when we were kids. He was the nicest guy."

Caroline didn't speak for a while. She rummaged in the fridge, eventually taking out a block of cheddar which she sliced thickly and ate just like that. "It's hard when these things happen," she said finally, "it's like lightning striking the house next door. It makes life feel so . . . fragile."

Olivier didn't say anything else. He didn't like when she did this, took a real thing and made it abstract. But he didn't want to fight. And Caroline didn't do well with guilt—she'd just end up twisting the situation to make herself the victim anyway. This was unfair of him to think, Olivier knew this. He had been thrown off balance by the news of Patrice's death. Everything in his apartment seemed wrong somehow, like they shouldn't be sitting there, eating cheese, talking about metaphorical tragedies when a real tragedy had just struck. He checked his phone. He was in a group chat on WhatsApp with all of the extended cousins. People had begun to send their condolences and to post old pictures of Patrice. He was in a few of them. Caroline came to sit beside him and he showed her his screen, pointing out all the family members by name and relation. She smiled and rubbed his back, glancing back at her own phone every few minutes. He stopped showing her pictures and began checking flights to Haiti.

"What are you doing?" he asked her, after she'd been quiet for a while.

"Oh, nothing important," she said, "I'm trying to remember this word I heard recently. It was a great word. German, I think. You know when you're walking in a park and there's the official path, but sometimes there's another path nearby, a natural path made from people walking over that spot again and again. You know what I mean? Apparently, there's a word for that. I'm trying to figure out what it is."

"Is this for a crossword or something?" Olivier asked.

"No . . . it was just bothering me."

"Man, these flights are crazy," Olivier said, mostly to himself.

"Flight?" asked Caroline, looking up from her phone.

"Yeah. I'd have to go through Phoenix, then Miami with an overnight. Wouldn't get to Port-au-Prince until Wednesday. I have that shift on Tuesday, but I'll have to miss it."

Caroline looked at him, her eyes squinted. She leaned forward and opened her mouth, as if to say something, then she shook her head and stood up, heading to the bedroom. "What?" Olivier called out, not following her.

"Nothing. Maybe we've got some miles you can use. Check our Aeroplan account." Olivier went to the bedroom and stood at the door. Caroline was arranging papers on her desk, organizing them into piles. A gnawing heat began to creep up his spine. His feelings for Caroline always seemed to teeter on the brink of tenderness and annoyance. Sometimes, in the middle of the night, he would roll over to find a stranger beside him and, for a moment, he would forget where he was.

Olivier watched as Caroline tucked a lock of thin blonde hair behind her ear, then licked the tip of one slender finger and used it to page through a stack of files, the movements studied and self-conscious. She had told him once that she had been bullied in high school by a group of girls who would invite her into their circle one week, only to shun her the next. He understood Caroline, recognized the stubborn way she occupied a space, like a dandelion emerging again and again from the same crack in the pavement.

He approached her from behind, cupping her elbows with his palms. He breathed her in, looking at where his fingers pressed into her forearms, her skin flaring red at the slightest touch. "That's not what you were going to say," he said finally.

Caroline sighed, and leaned into his chest. "I was thinking I could come too."

Every now and then they could hear the distant whirring of the Sky Train and the sounds of rush-hour traffic from the busy road a block away. Theirs was a nice apartment, by Vancouver's standards. Second floor, indoor parking. An actual building rather than a split-level of someone else's home. Their life, too, was nice. They made enough money to cover their rent and the occasional night out. They travelled, too. Malaysia. Tokyo. San Francisco.

Caroline hated that word "nice." She said he used it too often. "You're always saying so-and-so is 'nice' and this and that thing are so 'nice,' it doesn't mean anything." But Olivier didn't know what else to say. This was how he described Vancouver to his many aunties whenever one of them messaged him on Facebook. They always wanted to know what he was doing, so far away. Why he didn't live in Port-au-Prince or Miami or Quebec like his cousins. "It's nice here," he would say. And when they asked about his girlfriend, this Canadian girl they'd yet to meet, they would say, "She's a nice girl?" and Olivier would say, "*Oui, Tati, très gentille*. Very nice." And Caroline would cut her eyes at him, sucking her teeth like he'd taught her to, crawl toward him on the bed and say, "I'll show you how nice I am." He could never bring her to Haiti. The thought was sudden, like one of Caroline's metaphorical lightning strikes. But he couldn't shake it. He knew with his whole body he didn't want her to come.

"Yeah, we'll see what the prices are like," he said.

Caroline nodded, continuing to sort her desk, then said, "I mean, on second thought, do you think it's a good idea?"

"Maybe not," Olivier said, relieved. "You don't speak Creole and there will be so much family there. Plus, the vibe will be weird, with the funeral. It won't really be a vacation."

Caroline froze at the desk for a moment, and then recovered, shuffling the papers with extra vigour. "I meant maybe neither of us should go. We've got Shane and Emily's wedding in Toronto in a few months. And we just had to spend all that money on new brakes."

"I have to go. My cousin died."

"Second cousin."

Olivier laughed, a hollow bark, throwing his hands up and walking back into the living room. Caroline followed him. "You know what I mean," she said, "you'd have to cancel that shift and you could risk pissing off the foreman. You said you like this team and want to work with them again, right? Why jeopardize that?"

"Because my cousin died." He said it louder than he'd intended, enunciating each syllable. Caroline looked at him, and then at the floor, her arms crossed as if to protect herself. She jutted out her chin and wiped at her cheek, though it was dry. "I'm sorry," Olivier said, automatically. "I'm sorry," he said again, with more feeling this time. He pulled her to him, "I didn't mean to yell. I'm just upset, you know. It was so unexpected."

"It's kind of gross to use someone's death as an excuse to be an asshole," Caroline said, sniffing into his T-shirt.

A little while later, they sat together on the sofa and Olivier pulled up the flight search on his phone again. It really was expensive. And he hated layovers. Caroline sat beside him, hunched over her iPad. He figured she was sulking and expected to find her on Facebook, but when he glanced at her screen he saw she was looking at flights too. "What if you went out of Seattle?" she said, "I could drive you down. You'd still have to overnight in Miami but it's a bit cheaper." Olivier lay down on her lap, and she put the iPad down, stroking his hair instead.

"I don't know. Maybe you're right," he said, "I doubt anyone expects me to be there, anyway." Caroline played with his hair for few more moments and then reached for her iPad again. She let out a frustrated sigh, motioning for him to get up.

"What? Did you find something?" Olivier asked.

"Ugh. No. I just got this ridiculous email from the office. Listen to how passive aggressive this sounds." She read him the email then, her voice incredulous. She laughed a bit at the end and began typing her response, her nails clicking against the screen.

Olivier sat for a while, thumbing through his phone as more pictures of Patrice poured into the group chat. There was one of the two of them he particularly liked. Olivier looked about fifteen. He was in his Eminem phase then: baggy jeans, white tank top, buzz cut. Patrice was older, late twenties maybe, in jeans and a button-down. They were laughing, their arms around each other. A white chair lay toppled behind them. They'd been wrestling, Olivier remembered.

He thought of the grass against his skin, the way it was always a little wet even when it hadn't rained; colder than you'd expect for the tropics. Their neighbourhood was in the mountains and in the background you could see the garden, lychee and banana trees the only ones he recognized. He thought of showing Caroline the photograph, then changed his mind. He went to the kitchen. "What do you think about frozen pizza for dinner?" he asked, opening the freezer. He stood for a moment in front of it, letting the cold air dry the tears he didn't know had fallen. He stood until he could no longer remember what he was looking for.

More than a year later, Olivier will fly out of Vancouver airport on an airless August afternoon, the sky an oppressive white, the city choked by wildfire smoke. He will send Caroline a message before the plane takes off, a goodbye crowded with too many exclamation marks, too many emoticons to leave room for any genuine emotion. She won't reply before he turns his phone off, and by the time he lands in Port-au-Prince, he won't remember to check to see if she ever did. He will be picked up by his cousin, one of many cousins who feel like brothers and sisters to him and driven to his grandmother's house in the mountains. The drive will take them through the capital, that indescribable place, the side of Haiti you see on the news, the place his friends in Canada always picture when he talks about home. They will drive with their windows up through this chaos, the shanties, the garbage, the streets thick with too many humans in too little space.

When they reach the mountains he will take a deep breath that will feel like the first real breath he's taken in a long time. There, he will spend the next three days relearning the names of every tree in the garden, annoying his aunties with his constant questioning. What is this called? What is it used for? He will sing songs he thought he'd forgotten the words to, drunk on Barbancourt, his cousins laughing when, in the middle of the night, he lies on his back in the grass and tries to count the stars, always getting lost at fifty and having to start over.

LIGHTNESS

Joshua Wales

They called each other, respectively, Birdboy and Spaceman, which were nicknames they came up with while lying together in a single bed, the first night they slept together. Birdboy, because of his wide-open eyes, his delicate, angular face, and his short, slender frame that, as an adolescent, he would watch in the mirror, willing it to grow. And Spaceman, because he had always wanted—and still, in fact, wanted—to be an astronaut.

Spaceman confessed this to Birdboy with an endearing self-consciousness, while looking up at the map of constellations taped to the ceiling of his university dorm room. Astronaut training was an extremely competitive process, Spaceman told him, and the Canadian Space Agency only opened applications once every ten or fifteen years, so chances were slim. Birdboy, who was resting his head on the broad, dark-furred muscles of Spaceman's chest, had difficulty believing that someone with a jawline that strong could feel anything but a serene confidence in the inevitability of his aspirations— extraterrestrial or otherwise. Spaceman's height, the deepness of his voice, and the measured cadence of his speech all lent him a gravity that Birdboy felt he himself did not possess. Birdboy was sure that Spaceman, whose heavy hands made him feel significant in the way they gripped his ribcage, could feel his hummingbird heart through the smooth, pale flesh of his chest wall.

Four months later, it was December. Birdboy and Spaceman were sitting in the orange Formica brightness of a shawarma restaurant. They were taking a break from their residence meal-plan, watching out the window as snow brightened the early darkness of winter in Montreal. During a pause in their conversation, Birdboy became conscious of the ABBA medley arranged for solo cello that was playing overhead. He told Spaceman that perhaps he would take up the cello—an instrument he had always admired—and if Spaceman wanted, Birdboy would be happy to teach him, and then maybe they could learn some cello duets, and then take their act on the road, and then become famous.

Their cello future was offered by Birdboy in an offhand sort of way, playfully testing the direction of the wind that would carry them from present to future. This was Birdboy's first romantic relationship since a failed attempt at heterosexuality in the eighth grade, and the previous months had felt deeply correct—the way their gloved hands fit together, the way they talked importantly about Quebec politics instead of sleeping, the way they had sex seven times in twenty-four hours one weekend in late November. Birdboy had felt truly tethered for the first time; when he and Spaceman walked together to their classes, he had finally been able to feel his feet sink into the sidewalk. Indeed, it felt so correct that the question of their future was obviously and inevitably settled.

What Birdboy did not realize: in bringing up the future, he was flying into the coalmine of their relationship, unaware of the dark and tasteless air that threatened him. After leaving the restaurant, Spaceman looked down with his head of dark, snow-salted hair, put his gloved hands on Birdboy's shoulders, and said he was afraid it wasn't working anymore, he didn't know why, he was sorry, he didn't want to talk about it, maybe he'd see Birdboy around.

As Spaceman walked away, west along Ste. Catherine, Birdboy felt his body fade into a complete and terrifying weightlessness, until finally he was ripped up into the black atmosphere. He spun higher and higher. All he could hear was the alarm of rushing air in his ears, and all he could see were the blurred lights of the distant city. He was nauseated and vertiginous with the smooth violence of his ascent. He vomited on the pavement.

Later that night, wrapped in his duvet and looking up vacantly at the ceiling, Birdboy would tell his roommate, Sam, who had poured whisky into their chamomile tea, that he would never be completely happy again. This, Birdboy knew, was not an exaggeration.

Three weeks later, it was January. Birdboy was still in bed. He had not been able to access his inner reserves of guilt to propel him home for Christmas, and instead he stayed in Montreal, which his parents hadn't seem overly upset about, although his father had made him promise to attend Mass, which he had not. In fact, he'd left the residence building only a handful of times, mainly to pick up more dusty cereal and precariously dated milk from the convenience store nearby. Every stimulus he encountered in the outside world—the cold sun, the sound of car doors slamming, the faces of happy passersby—stung him, as if his skin had become porous and translucent, barely containing his vital organs.

January meant the beginning of a new semester. While Birdboy had intended to get to the first day of Introduction to Feminist Theory, his brain had, in the end, not seen the point. Instead, he cried, and napped, and tried to jerk off, and napped again, and cried. He pictured the faces of his classmates in the huge Brutalist auditorium in the centre of campus. They would be glowing a sickly orange in the fluorescent lighting, and their Ugg boots would be leaching out the salt, snow, and sand they had accumulated on the sidewalk, leaving tiny stalagmites of grime on the concrete floors. He pictured Spaceman in that auditorium, moving easily, trying to find a seat, charming strangers with his smile.

Later in the day, with the sun shining its accusations through the helpless blinds, he opened one of his required textbooks, which Sam had picked up for him at the campus bookstore. It was a collection of essays by Audre Lorde. He read the one about Lorde raising her son, and he immediately felt a deep jealousy at discovering that someone had *actually been raised by Audre Lorde*, the kind of mother that surely would have loved him. Birdboy's jealousy whipped itself into a rage when, after a bout of Googling, he discovered the name of Lorde's son, and that he had married a woman, and that he had become a banker. These facts made his brain hiss: *I would not have squandered Audre Lorde's parental love in that way.*

That Birdboy's own mother disliked him, he had discovered at age six, while he was playing alone on the church playground after Sunday school. He couldn't remember exactly what he was doing—certainly something performative, like a series of cartwheels, or a solo dance routine to Petula Clark's "Downtown." But when he looked over at the coven of mothers with their large-framed glasses and floral blouses, he found that they were laughing—not with a good-natured amusement mean, but rather with poorly restrained derision. A vicarious embarrassment. He watched his own mother press a hand first to her forehead and then to cover her eyes, in a gesture that he read unequivocally as shame. This was the kind of memory composed mainly of a feeling, and it was one he would come to know well: the nausea of levitation, the panic of floating out of control. He felt unable to secure himself, arms and legs flailing for a solid purchase. He reached for someone to grasp his diaphanous body and bestow on him the weight and substance of the other children on the playground, whose opaque bodies were kneeling in the dirt, carving worlds out of sand with their deliberate limbs.

If Audre Lorde had been there, she would not have held a hand to her eyes in embarrassment, she would have applauded whatever performance he had given, and run over to him, and embraced him. Her arms would have given him a real shape and form that he could propel, rather than watching, suspended, as the other children—then adolescents, then teenagers, then adults—flexed themselves through the world.

The sun on Birdboy's bed made his hands sweat. He closed the book, and closely examined Lorde's picture on the back cover.

He spent the following days and weeks in bed reading Lorde's other works—essays, books, and poetry that Sam brought home for him. He watched all of her interviews on YouTube, memorizing the tenor of her voice. Sometimes, when he slept, he dreamed about her. When he awoke, he felt somehow heavier. He tried to nap more often.

Eight weeks later, it was March, early morning. Birdboy walked in the dark rain toward the university, through the deserted Mont Royal Park, up the sloping sidewalk toward the angel statue. From a distance, he admired the concrete grace of this winged figure perched on top of the towering stone phallus, and wondered whether it was poised to fly toward or away from something.

He had not left his bed by choice. Rather, he was going to meet his academic adviser, who had emailed him the previous day to say: he was failing all of his courses, he'd missed too many classes, he was at risk of losing his scholarship, this was a serious matter.

At the pedestrian crossing at du Parc, he pushed the walk button and waited, marvelling at the speed and direction of the hundreds of cars that flew by.

A few seconds later the walk sign came on, urging him forward while compelling the traffic on either side to stop. Crossing quickly, he was awed by the long lines of vehicles that were just barely restraining themselves on his account. He paused, briefly, before reaching the other side, turning to face the oncoming traffic, testing their tolerance for his solitary figure. Their headlights glowered, reflecting off the wet pavement, and he felt the light pass right through his hollow bones and scatter him.

Ten years later, it is June. Birdboy is now sitting in Toronto, with Sam, in the window seat of a sushi restaurant. They are waiting for their food to arrive. In the intervening years, the content of their conversations has changed, but their roles have remained the same. Sam has listened through Birdboy's withdrawal from two masters programs and, with the authority of his medical degree, generously diagnoses personality disorders in the men who transiently populate Birdboy's sex life, including, most recently, a coworker at the queer bookstore who was composed exclusively of red flags. In return, Birdboy continues to make Sam laugh.

Now, Sam, with the enthusiasm of the hetero-monogamous, swipes on Birdboy's Tinder account on his behalf. As they have agreed, he rejects anyone with a neck tattoo, a picture taken at Macchu Picchu, or a selfie in or beside a car. Birdboy, meanwhile, describes the comedic premise of his idea for an iPhone app: Catholics could log on to confess, choosing from a drop-down list of sins—adultery, theft, *even sodomy* he pronounces with a stage-whisper and a hand clutched to imaginary pearls. The confessor would then receive the appropriate prescription for Hail Marys, or rosaries, or whatever, who really understands Catholicism. Sam laughs and continues to swipe with great concentration.

Birdboy will tweet about this app idea later. Not his best tweet, sure, but probably good enough to generate a greater-than-average number of likes. Recently, he acknowledged to himself with a grim, shrugging acceptance, that Twitter was one of his main sources of validation. He has now surpassed four thousand followers, which provides a satisfaction that, while not of the warming kind, at least adds to his weight.

Sam and Birdboy are suddenly interrupted by the slow, explosive stroll of Spaceman, who passes by the restaurant window. Spaceman's new salt and pepper beard makes his jaw even stronger and he has an infant strapped to his chest. He doesn't notice Birdboy, who folds into himself, hands covering his eyes.

Birdboy knew intellectually that this encounter was a possibility. He's followed Spaceman for the past ten years on an evolving landscape of social media. After all these years, checking on Spaceman's status was no longer a practice of passion, but rather of habit, like checking a horoscope. Birdboy has always been cheered by the banality of Spaceman's posts—a picture of him at his graduation from his PhD in some sort of engineering; wedding photographs with the clichéd navy and grey suits of all respectable gay grooms; an ultrasound of a baby, growing in an American surrogate who was, no doubt, being paid handsomely. Most recently, there was an announcement that Spaceman and his husband were moving to Toronto, after purchasing a house in the west end.

While for the most part, Spaceman's life updates have elicited only a pale, passing shadow of emotion, Birdboy was surprised by the anxiety he felt a few years back when he clicked on an article announcing the list of finalists for the Canadian Space Agency's astronaut training program, and then, by the profound relief he felt when Spaceman's name did not appear.

Spaceman has now disappeared from the window, but Birdboy remains still and contracted. Their sushi arrives, and Sam, who has also recognized this spectral intruder, squeezes Birdboy's forearm, releasing him. They break apart their wooden chopsticks, sand away any splinters by rubbing the two sticks together, and begin to eat in silence. After a few moments, Birdboy returns to the solidity of complaint—he cannot understand why no one saw the hilarity in his most recent tweet: "Hey Gogol, what is Russian literary surrealism?"

A few hours later, it will be nighttime. Birdboy will come home to his narrow, gable-roofed apartment in the third floor of an old house in the east end of the city. He will pass the Christmas cactus on the table at the top of the stairs, whose death he no longer registers. He will turn on a lamp by the futon. He will sit down. He will try to engage the cat curled up beside him, whose indifference, he has come to fear, is not actually feigned.

He will open his sex app and scroll through the matrix of side-lit torsos and bathroom selfies. He will scroll for a few minutes, hoping, as he always does, for something important to happen, which it will not. He will receive a message, but by this time of day, the thrum of the notification will no longer deliver a thrill of dopamine. *Hey daddy*, the message will say, followed by a photo of a disembodied ass in a yellow and white striped thong.

He will post the tweet about the Catholic confession and watch for several minutes as a light dusting of likes accumulates.

He will let the phone fall beside him. He will look up at the ceiling, and then at the cat. He will walk to the white light of the bathroom. The sink will be, as it always is, littered with the detritus of oral hygiene: light blue drools of dried paste, an empty container of dental floss, a rolled-up tube of toothpaste whose body he will have cut open with nail clippers, so that he might salvage the remnants that were too scant to be squeezed out the top.

He will take off his clothes. Most nights, he looks at himself naked in the mirror—sometimes with cruelty, occasionally with generosity. Tonight, however, he will look for the ways that he has changed since the last time Spaceman clasped his ribcage between his large hands. He will find, however, that he has remained largely the same. Slight-boned, translucent, hovering. He will begin to feel unmoored again, and his body will become so light that a thoughtless gust of wind could carry him precipitously upwards, battering his fragile limbs, until he is but a pinpoint in the sky.

SHINJUKU FOR STRAY ANGELS

Joy Waller

Mitsuo has a grey mind. Or silver. Cigarette smoke drifting among the neurons. "Coffee's too black," he tells me. "Coffee's too white. Ah. Yeah. I wish this was more like pearls. In-between shiny."

I think, too much acid.

He started too young, was probably the issue. Brain's still developing, up to a certain age—it alters your lens, when you take that route. There's a permanent detour, you can't find your way back. You *forget* to find your way back, no matter how many years go by. He fumbles stir sticks, this vibrating coffee shop in today's Shinjuku. Spills the creamer.

My coffee looks like fog.

*

Corduroy grooves on my face later when I wake up. It was Mitsuo's pillow case. It was textured. It sunk into me. It didn't want to go. But morning is firm. It's not morning. But I've awakened. It's an *ohayo* moment.

*

It's springtime. It's time to stop wearing boots. Edit them out. Replace them with flip-flops. On a Tuesday, sunlit, one of the flips loses itself, strays from me. Wanders away. It now resides, in solitude, in secret, somewhere on the sidewalk between Takadanobaba and Shin-Okubo. I walk one-foot barefoot for a while. When Mitsuo notices he gives me one of his flip-flops, the left one I think. Now *he* has been edited, flip-flop-cut, his narrative altered forever. A part of him has fallen to the cutting-room floor and the cutting-room floor is basically me.

I like this film.

But I worry about Mitsuo now. I'm concerned about his bare foot. I wonder what will happen if he steps on glass or rust. Neither of us are the sort of people that would cope too well with that. You could say we lack common sense. We keep walking for a while. A few weeks at least. When he leaves Tokyo and moves to Morocco we talk on the phone sometimes and lucid-dream Sundays together, if we're both free. But that's later.

*

My eyes gradually turn into pressed flowers. An indistinct, forgotten sort of blue. Mitsuo's are light-brown like two pinecones baking in the sun. He wants to go to a reggae bar. I don't, particularly, but we go. It's in a basement. Sweat. Iced coffee after iced coffee. White men in dreadlocks keep asking me to dance. Mitsuo spends 30 minutes standing in front of a speaker as big as a black hole, absorbing the vibrations, face ecstatic like a junk-sick monk. I go to the toilets for another quarter-hit. When I come back out Mitsuo is trying and failing to order a drink. That happens to him a lot. Language flees him, there's too much to keep track of. He holds the menu sideways and sort of shakes it at the bartenders, beseechingly. They probably think he's foreign. I worry a little about the police, their soft but visible presence in this city. We go soon. I buy him some vodka at the Family Mart. He seems a bit confused, but happy.

*

Somebody gives us a pineapple, I think it was his ex-girlfriend who is a waitress at the Pink Owl, and we slice it up and eat it and have sex and plant the top of the pineapple in expensive soil purchased from the home centre in Nakano, hang it from a basket on the steel railing outside my bedroom window. Mitsuo says it will grow into a whole pineapple tree someday. I wait a long time for this. Occasionally it strikes me that pineapples might not even grow on trees, they might come from something else. I water it every day.

*

I buy a pair of hot pants because Mitsuo says it would be very cinematic if I got some, red ones ideally, and wore them while doing mundane tasks such as putting stamps on envelopes and emptying ashtrays. It works out great. It actually does feel as though we are in a movie. Mitsuo stands at the kitchen counter peeling avocados and I bend over to place the pits in the garbage pail. The soundtrack is Puccini.

*

It's hard for me to show negative emotions on my face. It would be easier if I could fold myself, like origami. Like bedsheets. Instead, I simply sip my iced coffee. We're at Garlic Chips in Takadanobaba. Mitsuo looks distressed. I envy the way he can emote.

"Do you want me to cry?" I finally say.

"No," he says. And then amends it: "Yes. Or. Maybe. Just a little. But. Not sadly."

This is right after he tells me he's moving to Morocco, and wants me to come, too. In a little while we go to the Family Mart to buy mints. I always look around for my missing flip-flop, when I'm in this neighbourhood.

*

Tokyo at night. Skyscrapers shooting up to the stars, neon-eyed rats slinking through sewage drains. It's Hanami season so we go to Shinjuku Gyoen Park to look at the blossoms, but it's midnight and closed, the big steel gate locked shut.

"No problem," says Mitsuo. "There was no guard last year…"

We stuff our bags through the bars of the gate and then scramble up and over. A few steps farther there's another gate and we scale that one, too. And then we are alone in a vast inner-city park bathed in moonlight that an entire metropolis is locked out of. Mitsuo lights a joint. I touch the grass softly with my fingertips and say nothing as it begins to hum and vibrate, to writhe, to mimic breath in the same way I do. The entire place takes on an eerie, centuries-old glow. I feel like there are wolves around. The tree spirits let themselves be seen, and unseen. The twinkling neon lights of the city that frame and loom above the periphery of the park inhale, ponderously. They exhale. They groan and climax and think inane things. The trains of the subway howl like snakes below.

He kisses my neck and we walk along a narrow dirt path that leads, I am certain, to the instant of our conception. I look for it for a long while. Years now. I stock up on the necessities at Family Mart when I'm running low: chocolate, potato chips, tampons, iced coffee. I don't know why I'm looking. I just think it would be nice to find it.

*

"Maybe I could stay in Tokyo and be a waiter or something," Mitsuo says—a sort of faraway, doubtful look in his eyes. It's a bit of a stretch.

Jobs that Mitsuo has held in the past:
    baker
    organic farmer
    the guy who stands on street corners encouraging other
        guys to come into sex clubs
    tofu factory worker

That night is the final night and we go to a tofu izakaya in Shinjuku. He is softly critical of the waiters, whispers to me all the ways they could be doing it better, how he could handle a job like this no problem. But his heart isn't in it. Afterwards, we're still hungry so we go to Family Mart to buy cigarettes and pre-packaged salads. The sky outside is dark blue and the streets are slippery black. We don't feel lost.

METCALF-ROOKE AWARD 2021

Leon and I come at writing with vastly different rhetorics and strategies yet we also have much in common. We have read very widely in the short story form and we have pushed in our work at the story's shape, Leon, of course, far more than I. Yet despite the differences in our technical tool kits, we arrive at much the same judgements almost simultaneously. This year, quite independently, we each picked out what we considered the best five stories; our choices were identical in four of them. We moved then to the best three. This obligatory judging process was simply pro forma; we both had recognized that Colette Maitland's "Downsizing" was the inevitable choice because of the deep pleasure her pyrotechnic handling of language gave us. She delivered to us intensely realized characters and events through a dazzling verbal performance of great sophistication.

Language was the winner as we hope it will always be.

John Metcalf, Ottawa
Leon Rooke, Toronto

CONTRIBUTORS'
BIOGRAPHIES

Senaa Ahmad's short fiction has appeared in *The Paris Review*, *The Best American Science Fiction and Fantasy 2021*, and the *Pushcart Prize XLVI* anthology. In 2018, she attended the six-week Clarion Writers Workshop as the Octavia Butler Scholar. She's received the generous support of the Canada Council for the Arts, the Ontario Arts Council, the Toronto Arts Council, and the Speculative Literature Foundation. Her work was a finalist for ASME's National Magazine Award for Fiction and won the 2019 Sunburst Award for Short Fiction.

Chris Bailey is a commercial fisherman from eastern Prince Edward Island. He is a past recipient of the Milton Acorn Poetry Award, and holds an MFA Creative Writing from the University of Guelph. His work has appeared in *The Fiddle-head*, *Brick*, *FreeFall*, *The Antigonish Review*, and elsewhere. Chris' debut poetry collection, *What Your Hands Have Done*, is available from Nightwood Editions. Find him on Twitter and Instagram at @thischrisbailey.

Shashi Bhat's fiction has appeared in *Best Canadian Stories 2018 & 2019*, *Journey Prize Stories 24 & 30*, and other publications. She was the winner of the 2018 Journey Prize and was a 2018 National Magazine Award finalist for fiction. Shashi's second novel, *The Most Precious Substance on Earth*, will be published by McClelland & Stewart in Canada (Fall 2021) and Grand Central Publishing in the US (Spring 2022). Her collection of short stories is also forthcoming from McClelland & Stewart. Her debut novel, *The Family Took Shape* (Cormorant, 2013), was a finalist for the Thomas Raddall Atlantic Fiction Award. She is editor-in-chief of *EVENT* and teaches creative writing at Douglas College.

Megan Callahan is a writer, translator, book reviewer, and lover of languages. Her work has appeared in literary magazines like *Room*, *PRISM International*, and *Montréal Writes*, and her short story "Don't Speak" was longlisted for the 2020 Peter Hinchcliffe Short Fiction Award. Born and based in Tiohtià:ke/ Montreal, she is at work on her first short story collection.

Francine Cunningham is an award-winning Indigenous writer, artist and educator. A graduate of the UBC Creative Writing MFA program, Cunningham's work was shortlisted for the 2018 Edna Staebler Personal Essay, won the 2019 Indigenous Voices Award for unpublished prose, won the 2018 Short Grain Writing Contest, and she won the 2019 Lina Chartrand Award winner from *Cv2 Magazine*. She is a recipient of a Telus StoryHive Web-Series grant, and one of the 2018 Jenni House Artists in Residence in Whitehorse, YT. Her fiction has appeared on *The Malahat Review*'s Far Horizon's Prose shortlist, in *Joyland Magazine*, *The Puritan Magazine* and more. Her creative non-fiction has appeared in *The Malahat Review*, and *The Best Canadian Essays 2017* from Tight Rope Books. Her poetry has appeared in *Poetry Is Dead Magazine*, *Room Magazine*, *Hamilton Arts and Letters* and more. *On/Me* is her first book of poetry and has been nominated for the inaugural BC and Yukon Book Award Jim Deva Prize for Writing that Provokes and the 2020 Indigenous Voices Award in Poetry.

Francine has a book of short fiction, *God Isn't Here Today*, forthcoming with Invisible Press. You can find out more about her at francinecunningham.ca.

Lucia Gagliese is a writer and clinical psychologist. Her fiction has appeared in or is forthcoming in *The New Quarterly*, *The Healing Muse* and *Accenti Magazine*, and she has been a finalist in several creative writing contests including the CRAFT Short Fiction Prize and the Kalanithi Writing Award. She also has published extensively in medical and psychology journals about pain, ageing, cancer, and end of life care. She holds a PhD in psychology from McGill University and studied creative writing at The Humber School for Writers. She divides her time between New England and Toronto where she is a professor at York University.

Alice Gauntley is a writer of works that are literary, speculative, both, and neither. Her stories have previously appeared in *Plenitude*, *EVENT*, and *Grain*, among other publications. She lives in Tkaronto/Toronto, on the traditional territory of many Indigenous nations, including the Haudenosaunee, the Anishinaabe, the Wendat, and the Mississaugas of the Credit. Find her on Twitter @alicegwrites.

Don Gillmor's most recent book *To the River* won the 2019 Governor General's Literary Award for non-fiction. He is the author of a two-volume history of Canada, *Canada: A People's History*, which won the Libris Award, and two other books of non-fiction, *The Desire of Every Living Thing* and *I Swear by Apollo*. He has written three critically acclaimed novels—*Kanata*, *Mount Pleasant* and *Long Change*—as well as nine books for children, two of which were nominated for a Governor General's Award. He was a senior editor at *The Walrus* magazine, and his journalism has appeared in *The Walrus*, *Globe and Mail*, *Rolling Stone*, and *GQ* magazines. He has won twelve National Magazine Awards, including the Outstanding Achievement Award, as well as a National Newspaper Award. He lives in Toronto.

Angélique Lalonde is the second eldest of four daughters. She was raised on Ktunaxa territory and now dwells on Gitxsan Territory with her partner, two small children and many non-human beings. Angélique holds a PhD in Anthropology, is the recipient of the 2019 Journey Prize, and was awarded an Emerging Writer's residency at the Banff Centre. Her first collection of stories, *Glorious Frazzled Beings*, was published in September 2021. Her work has also appeared in several journals and the *Journey Prize Anthology*. angéliquelalonde.com.

Elise Levine is the author of the recent story collection *This Wicked Tongue*, the forthcoming novella collection *Say This*, the novels *Blue Field* and *Requests and Dedications*, and the story collection *Driving Men Mad*. Her work has also appeared in publications including *The Walrus, Ploughshares, Blackbird, The Gettysburg Review*, and *Best Canadian Stories* (2019, 2016, 2005). She lives in Baltimore, MD, where she teaches in the MA in Writing program at Johns Hopkins University.

Colette Maitland writes fiction, poetry and the occasional essay in Gananoque, ON. In 2013, Biblioasis published her first book, *Keeping the Peace* (short stories), which went on to be shortlisted for the 2014 Re-Lit Award. The novel *Riel Street* with Frontenac House came out the following year and was later shortlisted for an Alberta Book Award. Warm thanks to the OAC's Recommender Grants for Writers program, recommenders Biblioasis, *The New Quarterly* and The Porcupine's Quill, for their support of "Downsizing" and other stories.

Sara O'Leary is the author of a novel, *The Ghost in the House,* and numerous critically acclaimed books for children. "The

Ones We Carry With Us" is an excerpt from a longer work-in-progress.

Jasmine Sealy is a Barbadian-Canadian writer based in Vancouver, BC. She is a graduate of the MFA program at UBC where she won the 2020 UBC/HarperCollins Best New Fiction Prize. Her short stories have been published in *The New Quarterly, Cosmonauts Avenue, Room Magazine, Prairie Fire* and elsewhere and have been shortlisted for the Commonwealth Short Story Prize and longlisted for the CBC Short Story Prize. Her debut novel *The Island of Forgetting* is forthcoming with HarperCollins in Spring, 2022.

Joshua Wales is a writer and physician. His prose and poetry have been published by *Plenitude, Grain, The New Quarterly, Contemporary Verse 2, Globe and Mail,* and the CBC. He was a silver winner at the 2021 National Magazine Awards, a finalist for the 2021 RBC Bronwen Wallace Award for Emerging Writers from the Writers' Trust of Canada, and was shortlisted for the 2021 Commonwealth Short Story Prize. His work has also been shortlisted for *PRISM International* 's Jacob Zilber Short Fiction Prize, *CV2*'s Young Buck Poetry Prize, and won *The New Quarterly's* Peter Hinchcliffe Short Story Award.

Joy Waller is a Canadian writer and editor based in Tokyo. Her poetry collection, *Pause :: Heartbeat*, was released in 2019 (ToPoJo Excursions), and her fiction and poetry have appeared in *SAND, The Fiddlehead, Tokyo Poetry Journal, The Malahat Review*, and others. She is currently working on a collection of microfiction and literary fragments. For more information visit www.joywaller.com.

NOTABLE STORIES OF 2020

Helen Chau Bradley, "New Horizons"
Maisonneuve 75 (Spring 2020)

Kerry C Byrne, "The Doors That Do Not Open"
This Magazine (July/August 2020)

Kevin Chong, "Lottery Poetry"
The Walrus 27.6 (July/August 2020)

Joe Davies, "Invasive Species"
Queen's Quarterly 127.3 (Fall 2020)

Pam Dillon, "Murmuration"
The New Quarterly 154 (Spring 2020)

Cary Fagan, "Laughing Heir"
Geist 28.115 (Winter 2020)

Carmella Gray-Cosgrove, "Nowadays and Lonelier"
Freefall 30.1 (Spring 2020)

David Huebert, "Swamp Things"
The New Quarterly 155 (Summer 2020)

Jason Jobin, "Over Kawaguchi"
EVENT 49.2 (Fall 2020)

Zilla Jones, "The First Day"
Prairie Fire 41.3 (Fall 2020)

Ryanne Kap, "Heat"
Grain 48.1 (Fall 2020)

Conor Kerr, "Bridges"
The Fiddlehead 285 (Autumn 2020)

Emi Kodama, "A forest of houses, a corridor of trees"
The Malahat Review 210 (Spring 2020)

Stacy Penner, "When You See It, You Don't"
Humber Literary Review 8.2 (Fall/Winter 2020/2021)

Clea Young, "Hyacinth"
The New Quarterly 156 (Fall 2020)

PUBLICATIONS CONSULTED

For the 2021 edition of *Best Canadian Stories*, the following publications were consulted:

Brick, Broken City, Broken Pencil, Canadian Notes & Queries, Carte Blanche, Catapult, The Dalhousie Review, Electric Literature, EVENT, The Fiddlehead, filling Station, Freefall, Geist, Grain, Granta, Hazlitt, Humber Literary Review, Hypertext Magazine, Jewish Fiction.net, Joyland, Maisonneuve, The Malahat Review, Maple Tree Literary Supplement, Minola Review, Narrative Magazine, The Nashwaak Review, The New Quarterly, paperplates, The Paris Review, Plenitude, Prairie Fire, PRISM International, Pulp Literature, The Puritan, The Quarantine Review, Queen's Quarterly, Qwerty Magazine, Room, Strange Horizons, subTerrain, Taddle Creek, The /temz/ Review, THIS Magazine, Uncanny Magazine, Understorey, The Walrus, The Windsor Review, WordCity Literary Journal

ACKNOWLEDGEMENTS

"Let's Play Dead" by Senaa Ahmad first appeared in *The Paris Review*. Reprinted with permission of the author.

"What Would You Do?" by Chris Bailey first appeared in *The Fiddlehead*. Reprinted with permission of the author.

"Facsimile" from *The Most Precious Substance on Earth* by Shashi Bhat, copyright © 2021 Shashi Bhat. Reprinted with permission of McClelland & Stewart, a division of Penguin Random House Canada Limited, and Grand Central Publishing, an imprint of Hachette Book Group, Inc. All rights reserved.

"Good Medicine" by Megan Callahan first appeared in *Room Magazine*. Reprinted with permission of the author.

"Asleep Till You're Awake" by Francine Cunningham first appeared in *The Malahat Review*. Reprinted with permission of the author.

"Through the COVID-Glass" by Lucia Gagliese is previously unpublished. Printed with permission of the author.

"Stripped" by Alice Gauntley first appeared in *EVENT Magazine*. Reprinted with permission of the author.

ACKNOWLEDGEMENTS

"Dead Birds" by Don Gillmor first appeared in *The New Quarterly*. Reprinted with permission of the author.

"Lady with the Big head Chronicle" first appeared in *PRISM International*. From *Glorious Frazzled Beings* copyright © 2021 by Angélique Lalonde. Reproduced with permission from House of Anansi Press Inc., Toronto. www.houseofanansi.com

"Arnhem" by Elise Levine is previously unpublished. Printed with permission of the author.

"Downsizing" by Colette Maitland first appeared in *The New Quarterly*. Reprinted with permission of the author.

"The Ones We Carry with Us" by Sara O'Leary first appeared in *The Walrus* and was published in the 2020 Short Story Advent Calendar (Hingston & Olsen Publishing, 2020). Reprinted with permission of the author.

"Collapse" by Jasmine Sealy first appeared in *Room Magazine*. Reprinted with permission of the author.

"Lightness" by Joshua Wales first appeared in *Grain*. Reprinted with permission of the author.

"Shinjuku for Stray Angels" by Joy Waller first appeared in *The Malahat Review*. Reprinted with permission of the author.

ABOUT THE EDITOR

Diane Schoemperlen is the author of fourteen books, including eight short story collections. Her first collection, *Frogs and Other Stories,* won the 1986 Writers' Guild of Alberta Howard O'Hagan Award for Excellence in Short Fiction. In 1990, her collection, *The Man of My Dreams,* was shortlisted for both the Governor General's Award and the Trillium Prize. In 1998, her collection, *Forms of Devotion: Stories and Pictures*, won the Governor General's Award for English Fiction. Her most recent books of short stories are *By the Book: Stories and Pictures* (2014) and *First Things First: Early and Uncollected Stories* (2017). In 2018, she was awarded the Molson Prize in Arts by the Canada Council for the Arts "in recognition of exceptional achievement and outstanding contribution to the cultural and intellectual heritage of Canada."